The General Is Up

A Novel

Peter Nazareth

Goa 1556

2013

The General Is Up: A Novel
© Peter Nazareth 2013 peter-nazareth@uiowa.edu pnazareth05@msn.com
Published by

Goa 1556

Goa,1556, Sonarbhat, Saligão 403511 Goa, India
http://goa1556.goa-india.org, goa1556@gmail.com +91-832-2409490
Edited by Jeanne Hromnik in South Africa
Cover art by Steve Gronert Ellerhoff, Dublin/Iowa/Des Moines (author of
Time's Laughingstocks) stevegronertellerhoff@gmail.com
Cover design by Bina Nayak http://www.binanayak.com
Project coordination by Frederick Noronha
Printed and bound in India by Brilliant Printers Pvt. Ltd, Bangalore
www.brilliantprinters.com
Typeset in LγX http://www.lyx.org Text in Palatino

See Goa,1556's complete online catalogue at: http://bit.ly/Goa1556Books2

ISBN: 978-93-80739-65-6   Price: Rs. 200 in Goa. US$20 overseas.

*For
my grandson
Greyson
and
his parents Monique and Patrick*

Acknowledgements

J osé Antonio Bravo of Peru, Cyprian Ekwensi of Nigeria and Anthony Ocaya of Uganda acted as midwives to the birth of this novel.

Extracts have been published as follows: "The Institute," portions of Chapters 2 & 4, *Dhana*, ed. Ejiet Komolo, Makerere University/East African Literature Bureau, Vol. 4, No. 1, 1974; "Departure," Chapter 24, *OKIKE*, Special East African issue, ed. Chinua Achebe, Cambridge, Massachusetts, No. 10, May 1976; *Donga*, ed. Welma Odendaal, Westdene, South Africa, No. 8, March 1978; *Modern African Short Fiction*, Vol. III, trans. & ed. Satoru Tsuchiya, Taka-Shobo, Tokyo, 1978; *Literatura na Swecie*, trans. Jaroslav Anders, ed. Waclaw Sadkowski, Warsaw, Poland, No. 1 (81), 1978; *The Worker*, trans. Yitzhak Orpaz, Tel-Aviv, Passover, 1980; *The Toronto South Asian Review*, ed. Moyez Vassanji, Toronto, Ontario, Canada, Vol. 1, No. 2, 1982; Chapters 7 & 8, *New Quest*, ed. Dilip Chitre & V.K. Sinha, Bombay, India, No. 11, Sept./Oct. 1978; Chapters 11 & 12, *Pacific Quarterly Moana*, ed. Norman Simms, Hamilton, New Zealand, Vol. 4, No. 2, April 1979; *AL-IGHTIRAB AL-ADABI*, ed. S. Niazi and Samira Al'Mana, Sussex, No. 17, Jan. 1991; *Goan Association (U.K.) Newsletter*, ed. Alex Mascarenhas, London, Vol. 13, No. 6, March/April, 1980.

Grateful acknowledgement is made for the use of quotations to the following authors and publishers: Gabriel García Márquez, *No One Writes to the Colonel and Other Stories*, trans. J.S. Bernstein, Bard Books, Avon, New York, NY, 1973, p. 13 (permission granted by Harper & Row, New York, New York); Es'kia Mphahlele, *Down Second Avenue*, Doubleday, Garden City, New York, 1971, pp. 39/40; Christopher Okigbo, "Elegy for Slit Drum (With Rattles Accompaniment)", *Labyrinths*, Heinemann, London, 1971, p. 69; Ishmael Reed, *The Last Days of Louisiana Red*, Random House, New York, New York, 1974, p. 7.

The first edition of the whole novel was published by the Writers Workshop, Calcutta, 1984. The second edition was published by TSAR Publications, Toronto, 1991. I would like to thank the University of Iowa Foundation for their generous assistance. I would also like to thank Geoff Pope for setting up the type and for his editorial input during the preparation of the TSAR edition.

Power to Steve Ellerhoff, who drew the cover to the book while studying for his D.Phil. at Trinity College, Dublin. And to Jeanne Hromnik in South Africa for editing the volume; *Goa,1556* for digitising and publishing it; M.G. Vassanji and Nurjehan Aziz in Canada for permitting the new edition to be based on the one they had brought out previously; Bina Naik in Mumbai for the cover design; and the Golden Heart Emporium in Margão (Goa) for help in making the work materialise. Speaking of the power to make material: I greatly appreciate Frederick Noronha. For his vision, determination, persistence and skill without which there would be silence.

Peter Nazareth
Iowa City, Iowa
September 2013.

Author's Note

This novel is a work of the imagination, not a historical, biographical or journalistic record of facts, personalities or events. As such, all events, characters, ethnic groups and countries in the novel are fictional. Reference to any religion is in no way a denigration of people who are faithful to that religion: people are what they are, sometimes because of and, often, regardless of their religious affiliations. Any resemblance to real events, persons or countries is an unfortunate coincidence.

"You look as if you're dressed for some special event," she said. "This burial is a special event," the colonel said. "It's the first death from natural causes which we've had in many years."

–Gabriel Garcia Marquez,
No One Writes to the Colonel

... the way they related to one another, oppressed one another, maimed and murdered one another, carving one another while above their heads, fifty thousand feet, billionaires flew in custom-made jet planes equipped with saunas, tennis courts, swimming pools, discotheques, and meeting rooms decorated like a Merv Griffin Show set. The miserable workers were anti-negro, anti-chicano, anti-puerto rican, anti-asian...

–Ishmael Reed, *The Last Days of Louisiana Red*

The General is up ... the General is up ... commandments ... the General is up, the General is up, the General is up...

–Christopher Okigbo, "Elegy for Slit-Drum (With Rattles Accompaniment)" from *Path of Thunder*

1 He was coming in the dark, creeping up to the bed through the redness, creeping with a knife, with a machine-gun, with a grenade, until ...

"Get away!" The General sprang out of bed, gun blazing. "Plop, plop, crack, wram!!!!" Bodyguards burst in and turned on some light.

"What happened, your Excellency?"

"Who are you shooting, Bwana?"

"I was... I... Captain Oma was here with guns, knives, grenades!"

"But General, Captain Oma is...."

Yes, yes, it slowly came back. Pests were usually exterminated out of his sight: acid baths, beatings, shootings, tossing into the lake, he could rely on his men to do the job out of his sight and bring him the head. But Captain Oma was dangerous. He had helped the General overthrow the previous leader and now there were ambitions lurking behind those eyes ... so the General had to do the job himself. He had confessed that he was plotting with foreigners. The General was a big man and was able to break the arms and legs of the much smaller Captain. None of his predecessor's business of long trials, and lawyers, and judges, where the guilty man could escape after a lot of big talk. What was left of the Captain had been thrown into the lake. God had not made the crocodiles for nothing.

The General had become suspicious of all White people. They had once been his best friend; they had trained him, he had fought with them in neighbouring territory, and he had had a White pilot. But he had been persuaded by General Effendi to throw some of them out and since then they were out to get him. Like that accident of the petrol tanker at Blanwa, where two hundred people had burned to death. Sabotage. They were all over the place. And they were using Captain Oma.

The Captain was out to get him. The people kept seeing him in the country. He was organizing guerillas. The trouble was that the Captain did not accept him as the Rightful Leader, ordained by God to lead the country to salvation. Why not? Had not God sent him White men to push out his predecessor? Just because the man had been elected while he had come into power with a gun – that is, several guns supplied by friends! Well, the ways of God were strange, did not the people know? Was it natural to elect leaders or to have them chosen by God? Did the people elect leaders when the British had been in charge of the country, by the Grace of God? Ah, the people were stupid! It seemed that they wanted proof that he was indeed the chosen ruler.

The General re-loaded his gun and climbed back into bed, putting the gun under his pillow. He had given them proof. He had invited other Heads of State to visit him on equal terms and one had come, a Brother-General from a French-speaking African country. They had held fully-publicized ceremonies and named two streets and two lakes after themselves. He had loved ceremonies ever since he had served in the Allied army in the good old days when they were exterminating rebels; in recognition of his faithful soldiering, he had been promoted and given charge of the army before Independence. Ah, her Britannic Majesty was a great lady! A Great Lady!

But the visit of his Brother-General had not given him enough pleasure, not enough to blot out Captain Oma and all that blood. The French General was smaller but people thought he looked more impressive, all the way down his jacket. Hadn't the foreign newspapers said that he was dressed "like a Zanzibar door"? About himself, nothing! Why did they not say that he was dressed like, say, a Britannic door? Britain carried more honour than a tiny island like Zanzibar.

The General got out of bed and padded to the switch to turn on the light. He paced over to the cupboard and opened it. Ah, there it was, hanging by itself. Magnificent! The colours! The rich blue uniform – blue had always been his favourite colour. All his enemies had always turned this colour before being punished for their crimes. The white braid! The shiny black boots! No wonder so many women had married him, some even officially. The General began to put on the uniform. When he had put on his boots and cap, he looked at himself in the mirror. What was the word that French General had used in that funny language ... "Mag-ni-fi-gue!"

But wait, compared to that runt of a French General, he looked almost naked. He had hardly any honours, hardly any medals!

"Soolooomoooon!" the General shouted. "Solomon!"

"Yessir! Yes, Your Excellency!" The valet flung the door open, rubbing his eyes. "Did you call, my leader?"

"Solomon! A great man, appointed by God to rule over his people, must have proof of this responsibility! He should have all the honours this great country can give."

"Yes, sir! In fact, Your Excellency, the Council for Defence has already agreed to meet today, and I understand that they have decided to give you the honours of this country in the morning as a token of the esteem of the people."

"The presentation should be at the Governor's Lodge" – damn it, he sometimes forgot that the days of British rule were over – "I mean, at State House. The Minister of Public Affairs will be present with his photographers and reporters." He would show that short French pretender.

"Of course, General Excellency! I will personally see to it."

At 8 a.m. that morning, the Council for Defence decided that, as a small recognition of all that the General had done, he would be awarded all the top honours of Damibia. There were nine honours in all, including the Victoria Cross, a left-over from the days of British rule. There was no time to change the name to something more African. Anyway, the General loved those Queens. The soldiers decided to create one more honour for the occasion, Anti-Imperialism, First Class. That would round the figure nicely to ten.

The presentation was made at the State House. The speech was delivered by a civilian Minister, the Minister of Public Affairs. The Minister seemed to be suffering from a cold. He kept clearing his throat and wiping his face while reading the citation. The Minister said that all the honours were only a small token of the people's feelings: since the General had taken over, not one soul could say that he was unhappy.

The big moment. The chain bearing the honours was carried by the Chairman of the Council for Defence to the General on tip-toe – the Chairman was a small man. He had to struggle for some time to put the chain around the General's neck; you could not expect the Great Man to bow his head. Finally, the chain was on, the honours were round that head.

Flash! Click! Flash! The photographers were at work.

Snap! The chain had given under the weight and the ten honours had fallen in a heap at the General's feet.

"Sabotage!" howled the General. Blood began to appear before him. "The crooks! My enemies have done this evil thing! Shoot them!"

The Chairman had sprung forward and picked the medals and chain from the dirt at the General's feet. He and other members of the Council struggled to put the chain back round the General's neck.

"Cut their throats! Pluck out their eyes! Feed them to the crocodiles!"

"Your Excellency, Your Honour," quavered the Chairman, "the honours were unworthy of your expressive, honourable self! What honours from poor human beings can be suitable when God Himself had given you a Doctorate of Philosophy in Leadership."

The General was pacified and the Chairman struggled for a few more minutes, without success. It appeared that the chain was broken. The Minister of Public Affairs blew his nose and shook himself for a moment, saying, "Your Excellency, I know someone who can fix it! Give ... give me a moment." He disappeared, only to return a minute later dragging a man by the hand. The man was brown and unshaven and had a box in his hand.

"Excellency! Excellency! Anything happon? I you want, what for?" The man was transliterating from his native language.

"Who is this man?" bawled the General, springing back. "I said last night to the soldiers that all East Indians must leave this country! God told me so!" The General had received this message from God through a dream. Of course, he had known even before God spoke to him that these brown East Indians were dangerous. The B.B.C. had been full of the news that Her Majesty's Government had refused to let these people off the planes when they arrived in England. No wonder God had warned him.

"What is this man doing here?"

"Your Excellency ... "

The General leapt back, reaching for his holster and roaring, "What is he carrying in his hand?"

"Your Excellency," tremoloed the Minister of Public Affairs, "this is the State House electrician. He can fix anything that goes wrong at State House. He has his tool box here."

"That is right, Your Majesty!" the electrician said.

That pleased the General – that bit about the Majesty. Here was an East Indian who knew his place. If all the East Indians had been like this, why, who knows....

The electrician took a look at the chain, pulled out a pair of pliers, twisted a piece of wire round the chain, used a soldiering iron, and said, "Your Majesty! Ready! It can have fit for you!"

The chain was fitted round that head once more, and this time it stayed on.

"Make sure this man stays as long as he likes," said the General to the Minister of Public Affairs, who beamed with delight and nodded vigorously.

Photographs were taken again. They were all over the newspapers within a few hours. The newspaper had been delayed that day to carry the news of the great event. Within three hours, congratulations started pouring in from the country. Services of thanksgiving were offered.

Captain Oma did not trouble the General that night. The General slept bloodlessly.

2 "General say all East Indians must go from country soon
– this month!" Castro Viegas had burst into the bar of
the Lubele Institute with this announcement.

"What!" howled Ramos Pacheco, gulping down his fifth neat
whisky. "When did he say that?"

"T.V. Half-hour ago. I finished my work at Hotel early and
dressing when I heard. I came here soon soon."

"What did he say?" asked Ramos.

"He said God come, told him must rid East Indians. He
said God said East Indians dangerous."

"Ha, ha, ha!" laughed Joe Pereira, coming over and thump-
ing Castro over the back. "Look at Castro, trying to start off
another revolution! With such a crazy statement!"

Everybody at the bar laughed. They had got used to Viegas, although they did not see very much of him. He had just
turned up at the Lake Hotel nearby as a cook. Where had he
come from? Nobody knew. He told David D'Costa that he
had come from Brazil. He had gone to Brazil like most Goans,
thinking he could make his fortune there, but he had found in-
flation too high. He said he could not stand the uncertainty of
not knowing what the price of cigarettes would be every time
he went over to the shops. When drunk, he had told Gerson
Mendonca that he had worked at one of the most exclusive
White clubs in Rhodesia. He was sacked when the management finally found out that he was a Non-White instead of a
Portuguese from Mozambique: he had managed to fool them
for two years, he said, because he spoke fluent Portuguese.

Then he told Ronald D'Mello that he had worked in
Mozambique as a cook but he really was an underground agent
for Frelimo. But he was found out and tortured by the Portuguese. "Portuguese are bad torturers, worst in the world,"
he said. "Put me in cell of looking glasses, all six walls. I stand,
hands top of head, seventy-two hours. I gone crazy but my Frelimo comrades rescue me. Remember plane landing Leshona?
Three people giving up, asking political asylum? One is me."

The Lubele Goans never knew what to believe about Viegas. They were not even sure that he was a Goan because he
spoke English with a strange accent. "Bastard language," he
would curse when drunk. "No rules, everything stolen, just

like British people." They did not even know his first name. Joe Pereira noticed his resemblance to Fidel Castro, with his beard and moustache and ruffled hair, not to say his look of desperation, and gave him the name in recognition of his revolutionary affiliations. But nobody took him seriously. There was the time he used to complain that Old Man Fernandes, the senior cook at the Lake Hotel, was trying to sabotage him by putting potassium permanganate in the tomato soup, switching off the refrigerators at night so that the meat would go bad, mixing glue in the tartar sauce, and so on.

Ronald D'Mello, on an impulse while drinking at the hotel, visited Fernandes to find but. Fernandes's version was that Viegas envied him. "Goans don't like other Goans to get to the top," he said, adding that one day Viegas actually came for him with a carving knife during a long cooking session. "But I will not report Goans to the police," said Fernandes, looking proud of his moral superiority over Viegas. Ronald questioned one of the waiters. The waiter told him that no waiter would talk against Viegas because he would spend all his money on drinks and invite them to join in. But, he said, Fernandes was right. Viegas was only imagining things.

So now, people at the Institute bar were inclined to dismiss Viegas's words as just another of his unbelievable stories. It was impossible. Of course, the General was crazy enough to do anything; he had delusions that God had brought him into power, maybe because White men had helped him, and anything was possible; but that he should expel 120,000 East Indians in less than a month? The Civil Service, whose headquarters were in Lubele, would collapse. So would the whole economy. No, it was one of Viegas's stories.

In any case, most of the Goans at the bar didn't want to discuss the matter. They did not know whether some of the African members of the Institute had any relatives in the army. They could have wives who were related to the relatives of one of the General's many wives. Then again, there was Santan D'Silva, who worked as an electrician at the State House; he had a loose tongue and imperfect comprehension, so he could go back to work and say something against any Goan member, who could then be arrested or killed. George Kapa had already

13

gone home after the evening's tennis, but most Goans had the habit of being cautious about political matters unless they were absolutely sure there were no Africans around or they were absolutely drunk.

The group sitting on cane chairs in the far corner returned to its previous conversation. These chairs were made by Damibians to the specifications of Goans sixty years ago. They looked very Victorian with their high backrests but they had lasted and were much more comfortable than the newer bar stools.

"The trouble with David," said the tall and tubby Gerson Mendonca, looking like a bear from Sesame Street as he took a swig from his beer mug, "is that he likes Africans too much."

"What do you mean!" said Joe Pereira, sipping from a glass of whisky. The doctor had told him to cut down on beer because he was tending towards fatness. "What do you mean, too much! He likes Africans – I like Africans – but not every one of them. You like Goans, but you don't like all of them, as though we are only the dough in a large loaf of bread. Don't you have a running quarrel with Bruno Sequeira? The same is true of David and Africans."

"You know very well what I mean," said Gerson, ordering another whisky for Joe, even though he had not quite finished his drink. Joe made an effort to protest against yet another drink but gave up. There is nothing so oppressive as Goan hospitality. "Look at this Institute – our Institute," said Gerson. "A Goan Institute. We built it seventy years ago, when there was nothing in this country. With our sweat, our hard-earned money. Some of our parents even gave up a full month's salary to build it. Go and look through the records, available in the Institute store."

Gerson Mendonca was in his mid-forties and had come from Goa to join the Damibia Civil Service in the early fifties, when it seemed the British were the rightful rulers for all time. Like all the Goans of the time, he was very respectful towards tradition. The Independence of Damibia had taken him by surprise. But he knew it would never work and the coup had not surprised him. It irked him when people tried to break from traditional ways of doing things, people like David D'Costa and Joe Pereira, both in their early thirties. Gerson was a committee member when these two were children running wild, stealing mangoes and not even wearing shoes in the evenings.

"You youngsters do not bother to look through the records and then you think you are doing wonders for the Institute when actually you do very little compared to the elders. And what did David do? Last time he was President, he went and changed the name of the Institute to the Lubele Institute. He dropped the word *Goan*!"

"*He* did?" said Joe. "But surely he did not have the powers to do it! I thought the members of the Institute decided on the change of name. In any case, the Institute was already accepting non-Goans as members, so the members only regularized the position."

"The members didn't decide," said Gerson bitterly. "The members were blackmailed." It struck him that the word was most appropriate, and he laughed sarcastically. "Yes, *blackmailed*. None of the Goans at the meeting wanted to change the name. But George Kapa and Peter Langoko were there. Two Africans spoke in favour of the change and Goans were afraid to speak out against it. And David knew that was what would happen."

Joe Pereira felt his blood rising. Injustice of any kind always angered him and triggered him off, like pressing the starting button on a violent robot. He burst out, "But hell! You yourself were a member of his committee! You were a member of the very committee that took the decision to go to the general body of members with the proposal to change the name! Why didn't you speak then instead of now? I was only transferred back to Lubele six months ago, so why complain to me when you are to blame?"

"I *was* a member of that Management Committee," said Gerson. "But so was George Kapa. In fact, he was Vice-President. He and David connived at this plan and I was powerless to speak out."

Joe thumped his glass onto the table so hard it sounded as though it had broken. Heads at the counter turned in trepidation, wondering who was beginning a fight. "Why, in heaven's name? Why were you afraid to speak out? Kapa is a man, like you, like me. Would he eat you up? Would he arrange for you to be deported? You're just a damned coward, like most of the Goans around here."

"Joe," said Gerson patiently, "you're no better than David. Just because you are a citizen of Damibia, you think you are better off than us. Don't you know that you are an East Indian by classification? You and I might point out that we are Goans and not East Indians, but when it comes to trouble ... well, if it is true the General has decided to expel East Indians ..."

Ronald D'Mello, sitting at the counter, sensed trouble. He picked his long, thin shanks off the bar stool, walked to the table with a packet of potato crisps and offered the crisps to Joe and Gerson. Gerson had just started to say, "David likes Africans but you, Joe, you think you *are* an African ..."

"Why," said Ronald in a bantering tone, "look at my old friends enjoying themselves! Here, have a drink on me. Marcus!" – to the buck-toothed voluntary barman – "double-whisky for everybody at this table."

Joe was dangerously close to his limit and started protesting.

"Look here," said Ronald. "Don't insult me. It's my birthday and you cannot refuse a drink from me."

Joe Pereira vaguely recalled that Ronald had his birthday – when? – eight or nine months ago? Or was it six? He gave up the effort to think on his waterlogged brain and decided that it was less trouble to have the drink. By that time, Ronald had skilfully steered the conversation round to the volleyball game that evening against the members of the neighbouring Indian Club, which, surprisingly, had been won by the Goans. Joe and Gerson were still excited about the victory. As Ronald said, they had won thanks to Gerson's services and Joe's active net-returns. At closing time, Joe was standing up and demonstrating the backhand flip return that led to the winning point.

3 "The General of Damibia has done it again!" said the Editor-in-Chief of *The Onlooker* to the reporter.

"What?" said the reporter.

"The President-General of Damibia has just announced that all the East Indians in the country have to leave by the next moon," said the Editor-in-Chief.

"Damibia?" asked the reporter. "Where's that?"

"Africa. To be precise, Central Africa."

"What does 'the next moon' mean?"

"Who knows?" said the Editor-in-Chief, leaning forward in his executive swivel chair. "That's what I want you to find out. I want you to go over there and sniff out what is happening."

"Why me?" said the reporter uneasily. "Don't we have a man in those regions – what's his name – Simon Graves ..."

"Cecil Graves," replied the Editor. "But he is not very popular with the President of Damibia. You would have an advantage over him as a fresh man."

"But I don't know anything about Damibia," protested the reporter, looking out of the window at the reassuring London traffic congestion.

"See Jack Withers about it and he will give you some names to contact in Damibia."

"Maybe," said the reporter doubtfully. He had just come to work in London from Skipton, Yorkshire, and found London dangerous enough without going to the wilds of Africa.

"Come on, Alan!" said the Editor-in-Chief, wearing the armour of his Oxbridge accent. This was always a useful weapon against these fledgling reporters from the North. "Africa isn't half as dangerous as, say, Vietnam. We taught them during our years of rule, we gave them our own rule-of-law and a written Constitution. This is a god-sent chance to break into the big time. Reputations are made overnight by brilliant reporting over African affairs."

"All right," said the reporter, trying to sound convinced but looking worried.

"Here is a handbook on Africa by Victor Ulture, an authority in the field. Look up Damibia. And get ready to leave tomorrow at the outside."

That night, sitting in his apartment in Shepherd's Bush, the reporter looked up the section on Damibia in *Ulture's Handbook*. He read:

Land Area: 121,487 square miles.

Geography: A Central African country, it is formed mainly of a plateau 4,000-4,500 feet above sea level, some peaks rising to 5,500 feet. It is bounded on the north and north-west by Zaire, on the south and south-west by Aziland, on the south and south-east by Leshona, and on the east by Mozania. Shares Lake Elizabeth, the second-largest lake in Africa, with Aziland, Leshona and Mozania.

Climate: Three seasons: Rainy from October to March; cool from April to August; warm and dry from August to October (60°F to 70°F).

Population:

Total population: 13,645,381 (1968).

Rate of growth: 3.5%.

Non-indigenous population: 7,117 Europeans; 121,819 East Indians or people of East Indian origin (including 5,079 Goans).

Main towns: Blanwa (capital), 550,716; Lubele (administrative capital), 27,163.

Language: English is the official language.

Religions: Roman Catholic, 29%; Anglican, 27%; Muslim, 14%; traditional religions, 18%.

Armed forces: About 19,000.

Education:

School attendance rate: 45%-50% (1968-69).

Primary: 1,157,006 pupils.

Secondary: 68,561.

Teacher training: 6,118.

Technical: 4,909.

Higher education is carried out at the University of Damibia, 3,142 students; there are 3,827 students abroad.

Public Health: 81 hospitals. 1 doctor for 10,297 inhabitants.

Information:

Radio and Television: Radio programmes are broadcast in English and in the main languages of the country. Studios in Blanwa.

Press: One daily, *Daily Damibian Times.*

Roadways & Railways: 21,388 miles of road (2,105 mile tarred); 998 miles of railway track.

Agriculture and Mining: Main exports (1967): cotton, 764,059 bales; tea, 47,311 tons; cocoa, 28,157 tons; groundnuts, 18,000 tons; tin, 29,471 tons.

Gross National Product: Global (1968) – 350 million pounds sterling.

Standard of living:

Cars: 47,331.

Telephones: 37,491.

Cinemas (1966): 37.

Radios: 180,771.

Televisions: 13,404.

Monetary system: Shilling and cents (26.118shs.=1 pound sterling).

History: Together with Leshona and Mozania, Damibia was under British rule. It received Independence on July 23, 1963. The first Prime Minister of Damibia was Paul Mbuyiseni, later President when the country was declared a republic on March 15, 1965.

Form of government: Parliamentary form of government until April, 1970. The regime of left-leaning Mbuyiseni was overthrown by a military coup.

That doesn't look too bad, thought the reporter. The cars and the roads and the religions and the standard of living made Damibia sound like it could be quite a comfortable place. He had some doubts about the military government; but then, the previous government had been left-leaning and so the new one would probably be friendly to the British. He vaguely recalled reading some time back how pleased the people were when one leftist African leader was overthrown while he was at a Commonwealth Leaders Meeting abroad. The British papers had seemed pleased about it. Could this have been the leader of Damibia?

The climate would be like summer, the summer all Englishmen longed for but seldom got. It was already beginning to turn cold and the heating in Shepherd's Bush was not adequate, what with these electric and gas heaters. Back in Skipton he used firewood in the fireplace, which warmed the whole body instead of just the front, like these miserable electric things. And there was the bonus of making a journalistic break. Why, this trip might actually be enjoyable and profitable!

He picked up the phone and dialled.

"Jack Withers? This is Alan Mansfield. Yes, Mansfield. I work with *The Onlooker* too. I am being sent by the Big Chief to Damibia and I understand that you are an expert on African affairs. I wonder if you would be kind enough to give me some names to contact when I am in Damibia."

4 At closing time, some members had to help Castro Viegas to one of the cars. He seldom came to the Institute, but whenever he did he had so many drinks that somebody or other had to help him home. Of course, there was always a bonus in this charitable action – he would invite them into his place and offer them some of the hotel stock lying around his room. Martell was not a brandy one could afford every day, even at the Institute rates.

Ronald D'Mello decided to walk home for a change instead of asking one of the old regulars for a lift. In fact, he had to positively sneak out or else he would have had to explain why he wanted to walk. For that matter, he did not know why he wanted to walk. Perhaps it was just to clear his head. He had drunk more than was good for him and thought he would not be able to sleep if he went straight home. Neither did he feel like trying the alternative, namely, looking for a woman, as he and some of the other fellows did occasionally.

No, he just wanted to walk and feel the cool air on his skin and bones. Mmm, delicious cold! But not as chilly as in some parts of India, where the cold penetrated to your very marrow. This one made him feel real and somehow there, present. He heard a zz-zz-oooom behind him, suddenly saw lights, and – "Bastard!" he exploded as he jumped out of the way of a speeding car and landed in the gutter. "Another one of those affluent bums who can't wait to get to the airport!" he thought, half-enviously.

Picking himself out of the gutter, he wished at that moment that he could go to the airport and leave Lubele and all of Africa behind him forever. But then, if what Castro Viegas had said was true, perhaps he would have to do that. Not that he believed Castro. Oh, he knew that all East Indians who were not citizens of Damibia would have to leave some day, but he was a Damibian citizen and would stay. Surely the General would not expel East Indians who were citizens too – he could not. But then, he could do anything. Hadn't he killed so many Damibians, without a trial? Like most of the people in Abala, Ronald had stopped eating fish because too many bodies were being found in the lake. Who knows what the fish ate?

He saw lights of the rows of houses by the side of the road as he walked up the hill. They brought back memories of his youth. He was born in Abala where his father had worked as a civil servant, and he had also been to primary school here. Though, after the fashion of his time, his father had refused to send him to the secondary schools in the city, Blanwa, because they were Indian and, by definition, inferior. He could not go to any of the Damibian secular or mission secondary schools because that was not the done thing, and besides, the colonial government had made sure that there was no racial mixing, no pooling of resources of the Non-White peoples. So he had gone to study further in Goa, where he had discovered that there was nothing inherently middle class about Goans. Just like Damibians, Goans could be servants, bus drivers, peasants, as well as the occasional landowner.

"Such a fuss about the name of the Institute!" he said aloud. As though the Institute defined the essence of Goans for all time instead of being a creation during the colonial period of Divide-and-Rule! Were there any Goan Institutes in Goa? He had looked for Goan Institutes when he had first arrived in Goa but had not found any. Of course the name had to be changed. He had supported David's proposal wholeheartedly and had spoken in favour of it, to the annoyance of Gerson Mendonca. He said that it should have been changed earlier so that it could have provided a window into Goans, so that Goans could at least be known and so that Goans could know Damibians.

Who is not suspicious of the strangers in one's midst when one does not know them, he thought. When the fighting for Independence had gathered momentum in Goa in the fifties, he had seen with his own eyes that the Portuguese were on the run – that is, until they brought in African troops from Mozambique and Angola. The Goan people had been really scared of these unknown black soldiers and got so disheartened they gave up.

He walked past the middle-class houses, rather, lower-middle-class houses, all belonging to the government. The houses had seemed so solid and so mythical in the days of his childhood. Lubele was the whole world, each house seemed an extension of the people who lived in it. No, each house looked like the people who lived in it. Don't psychologists accept that after a few years of marriage husband and wife begin to look alike as they adjust psychically and plastically to each other? Well, why must one assume that this only happened between human beings and not between human beings and houses?

One could say, "There is the house of Rosario Mascarenhas," with a high forehead and a sloping top. He was thinking of the Goan houses. Far away there were the mansions provided with the moat of a wide compound, a fence, and probably a dog or two. The Europeans did not so much live in them as disappear into them, like angels going into heaven. The Englishman's home in Lubele was truly his castle.

The lights of the house he was walking by went out. It was Louis Lobo's. "They're feeling randy tonight!" thought Ronald, obscenely. "It's time for their weekly fuck. Everything according to a time-table. That's the story of the petty-bourgeois civil servant." He cursed, and added another curse because, for all his education, he too was a civil servant. God knows why he had chosen to come back to Lubele after graduation in India. His father had been about to retire and settle down in Goa. Funny about that "down in Goa" bit – one was always "going down to Goa". Was this an unconscious recognition by the Goans that they, the Africa "Goacks", led an inferior life in Goa, speaking economically?

Maybe his returning to Africa was just the habit of Goans doing whatever their fathers did, a survival of caste behaviour. One followed the line of least resistance. Or maybe it was a more profound impulse – one had to go back to the place of one's youth and early memories. He suspected, though, that it was really because he loved Africa, loved the greenness of the smell, loved the people who were what they were and, except for the General, did not pretend to be otherwise.

He had heard all the awful things about Damibians when he was very young: that they were unreliable, that they could not stand criticism, that they were inferior, that they were immoral, and so on. He had half believed all this. Then he had gone to Goa and found the same things said by the Portuguese rulers about the Goan peasants while in Damibia the rulers had nothing but praise for the Goans. He had come to suspect that all rulers must try to justify their position. When many Goans said that they were born to be servants, thus explaining the fact that they did not rule themselves, he knew that the rulers had succeeded in entering the minds of the conquered.

We're caught in a trap. Blaring out from the house he was passing. *I can't walk out.* Elvis Presley with "Suspicious Minds". Ronald's sentiments. It was the daily late-hour request programme. "Suspicious Minds" was popular in Damibia because it had a touch of soul as well as country 'n western. Ronald wondered why both Goans and Damibians loved country 'n' western, music of people halfway across the globe; maybe it was because it expressed the feelings of people struggling to make a life, with no frills. This house, which once was indelibly Goan, was, incredibly, occupied by a Damibian. How did the Damibian get on with his Goan neighbours? His car, a Mercedes-Benz, was in startling contrast to their economy-sized cars, and no doubt they had commented on it among themselves, feeling virtuous that they did not squander their money like the Damibians.

Ronald once again said, "Bastard," cursing the unknown African for wasting his money on a petrol-guzzling, tyre-chewing Benz, and then added, "Bastards too!", cursing the Goans in Damibia who hoarded almost every cent, as though the whole aim of life was to accumulate every coin and note. Though the one wanted to hoard it and the other to spend it, Goan and Damibian were two sides of the same coin in their excessive devotion to money.

Suddenly, Ronald was nowhere. The street lights had gone off. It was midnight and, from colonial times, the lights were always switched off at that hour. The darkness was all around him – like a Damibian woman, he thought. After all, he would like a woman to warm his bed. The impenetrable darkness had reminded him that he was lonely. And if what Castro Viegas had said about East Indians having to leave within a month ... well, he was not so sure; Viegas appeared crazy but he sometimes seemed to know much more than the cocooned civil-servant Goans, whose world was perimetered by chapters from the Government Standing Orders. Maybe he spoke as funnily as Santan D'Silva but there was no comparison between what they thought and experienced. Anyway, if what Castro had said was true, he had better get himself a Damibian woman before the news got around. Who knows – later, maybe, the Damibian women would not like to endanger themselves by being seen with East Indian men. It was not safe to go against the orders of the General, as so many had found out to their cost and the advantage of the crocodiles.

Ronald decided to retrace his steps towards one of the Damibian bars and find himself a woman. Lubele was a singularly lonely town; in the city it would be easy enough to meet a woman at a nightclub, but here it was not so easy, what with all the Goan bachelors like himself and Joe Pereira on the prowl. The Goans were very Victorian. Their girls were expected to be respectable and straight-laced and anti-sensual. The result was that the honest men had to hunt out Damibian women who did not have the Goan problem (the dishonest ones could find bored housewives, tired of their arranged, loveless marriages to older, respectable men or the more daring ones whose defiant love marriages had dried up all too soon).

Ronald was no saint. He liked women. But he didn't like this money business, this paying of the woman for services rendered. He was a romantic at heart and wanted his women to have some, well, love for him. This happened only occasionally, with one of the new secretaries from England or one of the visiting air hostesses. He had thought that he would be able to fall in love and get married when he had gone to Goa on leave a few months earlier. A man from Africa was always flooded with proposals because he was supposed to be "well off". Well, one could always fall in love with a beautiful girl, and if there was a dowry to go along with her, why should he say, "No."

In the event, he had no chance to fall-in-love. By the time he was in Goa on leave, word had got around that the future of Goans in East and Central Africa was very uncertain. Some people had heard of the East Indian Census held by the General a few months after the coup and they figured that no good could come of it. Ronald did not receive any proposals worth considering. The only accessible attractive girls preferred American hippies to him. He had even tried to act as a hippie for a while but his brown skin had been a dead give-away, all the hippies being the children of rich white Americans.

So he was back in Damibia, still single and searching at this unearthly hour of the night for female company. He walked slowly down the tarred main road, savouring the damp night air. He was past the Lubele Institute, which looked like some deep-sea monster fast asleep, and was walking towards a smaller building, the Indian Club, belonging to an earlier era because, unlike the then Goan Institute, it had never been extended or improved. In other towns and cities in Damibia, the various Indian institutions were magnificent, but here, where the only Indian businessmen permitted by the colonial government were ones needed to service the civil service headquarters, the lone Indian Club reinforced the colonial image of Goans as different from and superior to the Indians.

Of course, Goans felt superior to those money-grubbing Indian businessmen for they, the Goans, were serving the government. The Indians for their part – with the exception of the few who were civil servants – despised Goans for being in service occupations instead of being self-employed. But both agreed on one thing: they were both superior to Damibians.

"We are all children of Divide-and-Rule," thought Ronald. Strange, he wondered, as he walked past the Indian Club, looking pathetic beside its bigger brother. India had a visible history extending thousands of years and one thought of the past fifty years in India as only a wrinkle on the face of Father Time. But here in Africa, a building fifty years old seemed to belong to neolithic times. Was this because colonialism had destroyed the Damibian people's sense of the past much more than it had done in India? Or was it that Ronald himself could only think a few years back in Damibia as he was of "immigrant" parentage"?

He heard the piercing drilling of hundreds of crickets and, above it, a sound similar in some ways, notes drifting across the swampy air from Akede's Arizona Nightclub. Lights, cars, sounds of laughter – and wham! he was in a different world, all sound and laughter. He walked up to the counter and ordered a beer. It was slightly more expensive than in the Goan Institute because here one paid commercial rates. People looked at him for a second – it was not usual to see an East Indian or Goan at their bar, more so as it was not considered a high-class bar by the elite. But then, people did not ask questions. All those who wanted to come and enjoy themselves were welcome. And the few intelligence agents around would not mind; they needed to earn their keep.

Pretty soon, a tall, Caucasoid black woman wearing an ankle-length, flowery kitenge moved towards him. She probably once wore a micro-mini to exhibit her wares but had to cover up when the General banned minis. Still, she wore a blouse so tight that Ronald could not breathe. She had big tits that reminded Ronald of the volleyball game that evening: they bounced like crazy as she moved. She was at his side, asking him to buy her beer. Of course he did. She said her name was Jane and asked him his. He was tempted to reply "Tarzan" but instead said, "Gerson Mendonca." Would that surprise the prim and tight-arsed Ethel Mendonca when she heard through the grapevine that a woman of the night claimed to have serviced Gerson Mendonca! No, this Jane would know Ronald was lying about his name because all East Indian and Goan civil servants pretended to be virtuous. And she could always find out his real name if she wanted to.

They made small talk over the beer in broken English and "pidgin" Swahili. She asked him whether he wanted to dance. He did, and they swayed in front of the jukebox, a standing simulation of the main business of the night. They went back to the bar counter and he ordered two more beers. She drank hers much faster than he did. African women loved beer while Goan women had to pretend they didn't like the stuff – it was unladylike to say that they did, though many were secret beer drinkers.

After another dance and beer, the woman asked him whether he wanted some comfort. He nodded. She named her price. He said he wanted her for the whole night. She named a second price. He made a perfunctory effort at bargaining; after all, she could see that he would not trouble her for the whole night with all the booze in him and then she would have the bonus of sleeping in a soft-mattressed bed. Besides, this was part of the game; part of the whole business of shopping was to bargain, and only American tourists did not do so. But he soon gave in, adding that she would have to walk two miles to his place. He thought she might object because there was always the risk of a drunken soldier or two on the loose but she went to get her bag to leave.

There was nothing like a Damibian woman, Ronald thought. She would give him his money's worth and enjoy herself too, without verbalizing her desire. The European and American women had an obsession about talking of their sexual desires and feelings. It was as though they needed words to convince themselves that they were feeling the man's tool inside them, as though orgasm could only be so if it could be put into words. The only thing was that this Jane would certainly not do any of the fancy stuff liked by the civilized white people, like fellatio, sodomy, etc., but that was okay with him. He had no quarrel with the way nature had made human beings.

The woman and he made some small-talk all the way back home, walking hand-in-hand. The darkness all around felt comforting and Ronald was gradually absorbed into a black womb...

5 George Kapa returned home early after only three beers at the Damibia Institute. He had had a very satisfying game of tennis, and Damibian beer was just the thing to cool off his thirst. He had travelled all over the world – he was a water engineer at the U.N.-aided Hydrological Research Centre at Lubele – but nowhere abroad had he tasted beer as good as one could get in Damibia. Must be the Damibian water, which was in pure and plentiful supply. No wonder Damibians were such heavy drinkers!

Normally, after a few beers and a game of darts at the Institute, he left and went over to one of the African bars or to Silva's Moonshine Bar, run with an African atmosphere by a slightly disreputable Goan whose brother was the State House electrician. George liked the company of Goans, but only for so long. They were not uninhibited enough for his liking, and they seemed to respect rules too much – whether the rules of the government or the rules of society. Some of them, like Gerson Mendonca, were not open enough with him because they were afraid of his power as one of the new breed of university-trained Africans. They also seemed to think that because he was a Damibian he was politically powerful. This was not the case with David D'Costa, but then, he and David had studied at University together whereas most of the other Goans were civil servants from British times.

George was sometimes irritated by Goan hypocrisies. For example, he knew, although most Goans were very careful not to talk about it with him, that Goans thought that the main problem facing Africa was tribalism. They seemed to exempt themselves from the whole problem, as though they were not tribalist in their behaviour. Just as there was a tendency for the Ganda to look down on, say, the Lwo and to ascribe some tribal characteristics to them, so also did the Goans look down on, say, the Hindu Patels, thinking of them as a small-minded people concerned only with making money. Even more ridiculous, Goans were at such pains to point out that they were not Indians and most of them were still angry over the Indian takeover of Goa from the Portuguese, instead of being pleased that they were freed at long last from one of the most vicious of imperialists!

On the other hand, George had to admit that Goans were different from Indians. For instance, they spoke English and very seldom spoke their own language. When Indians spoke in Hindi or Gujarati in his presence he could not help feeling insulted, as though they were making plans to cheat him. Then again, Goans were Catholics, and although he did not go often to church, he admired people who did. Goans were very hospitable and he received any number of free beers from Goans in the Institute bar. No doubt a little of this had been due at the beginning to their fear of his alleged power, but now he knew that they really meant it as friendliness. And when they had all had a few beers together, they spoke to one another with real warmth and little reserve. Again, the Goans were financial wizards at running this Institute on a shoe-string.

This was what had drawn George Kapa to the Lubele Goan Institute in the first place. He was a Karamoli from the west of Damibia, and when he was posted to Lubele, a stronghold of the Gembe, he had felt that he was in slightly foreign territory. He had always been fond of tennis – he had represented the University at tennis – and so he had looked around for a tennis club. He had found three clubs that offered tennis: the former European club, the Lubele Goan Institute and the Indian Club. He found that the Lubele Club, which had never included the word "European" in its title, was now completely open to people of all races, but the fees were very high, no doubt to discourage undesirables from joining.

The entrance fee to the club was Shs.300, thereafter Shs.50 per month plus Shs.30 per month for tennis. The Indian Club looked too grubby and little used for his taste. As for the Goan Institute, he found that the entrance fee was Shs.100 and the monthly fee was Shs.10, inclusive of tennis and any other games he wanted to play. Furthermore, the drinks at the bar were cheap. How did they manage this? He found out after he joined that it was the same careful management that the Goans used when they looked after the finances of the Government. They ran a few big public dances during the year on which they made a profit with which they could buy bar stock, tennis balls, etc. The bar was run by a member of the Institute on a voluntary basis, with a percentage of the bar profits as his honorarium to supplement his small civil servant's salary. Oh, there was a little pilfering occasionally – people always cheated their own kind, although they made a fuss about the smaller cheating by the servants – but it was very little. It seemed that even in dishonesty Goans were honest; or maybe they could only think small.

George was sponsored for membership by David D'Costa, who was determined to open up the Institute to African members. George knew that David thought the Institute had a moral obligation to be totally open, now that the racist colonial rule had ended. Also, George suspected David knew that if the Institute were not voluntarily open, history would force it to; and it was safer to do it voluntarily. As George discovered, the Institute was the life and soul of the Goans, whereas for him it was merely a place where he could have his tennis, darts, drinks and some relaxation. Still, George wanted the Institute to be completely open. He wondered why the general meeting of the members had only changed the rules and not the name. Was it only hypocrisy, to keep the Institute open only in theory, knowing that non-Goans would not be attracted because of the name? But no, in that case, they would have done like the Europeans, having a clean front and placing obstacles behind. Two years later, David himself stood for election as President and won. David then asked George to come in as Vice-President, the first African Vice-President of the Lubele Goan Institute.

George had refused. "How can I become Vice-President of a Goan Institute?" he said. "The name is not appropriate any more. The other day, when we played a tennis match, the Blanwa Lions captain said, 'Where is the Damibia Goan Institute team?' and I said, 'Here we are,' and there we were, two Damibians, one Indian and one Goan! It's not right."

"That's exactly it!" said David. "Come in, and we will go to the general meeting of the members and ask for a change of name. When the rules were changed I proposed a change of name, but all the older Goans present were sentimental. The younger ones were afraid. They had not forgotten that, in colonial times, older Goans took out Institute disagreements with younger members at the office, denying them recommendations for promotions, etc. They thought those who had suffered through this must now be waiting for their turn to do the same to others! If you come in we can try again to change the name, and if we fail you can resign. But we will not fail. Enough of the younger members back me over this issue."

So George had come in, and he, David and the younger members like Ronald had planned it: they made sure the issue was discussed openly and that there was no secret ballot, on the grounds that the Institute was very democratic, like Damibia itself (that was before the coup). The older members, including Gerson Mendonca, who was a member of the Management Committee, were afraid to speak out or to be seen voting against the change of name, and the name had been changed. But life carried on at the Institute very much as usual; it was still primarily Goan in spirit and behaviour.

Sometimes, George was puzzled by David. They had been friends at University, where they had shared the same hall of residence. David did not have the hang-ups of most Goans, the tendency to stereotype. He was too intense about everything he did, and he did many social things, never seeming to relax and be light-hearted. David was very African in being serious about responsibility, very African in being open-minded and not looking for inflexible rules.

For instance, David had been persuaded by George to stand as Chairman of his hall of residence, the oldest one in the University, and he had won, although there were only a handful of Goans and East Indians in the hall. He did not spend much time at dances, and he never seemed to have played sex with any women while at University, while other East Indians and Goans had used their greater wealth to get as many Damibian women as they liked, clannishly making sure that none of the Damibian men could get their women. Even when he drank at the bar, David seemed to drink in moderation and always made his escape before he could get drunk.

George was much more easygoing than David, particularly regarding women. According to his upbringing, it was no big deal having sexual affairs with willing women, provided they were not married; Puritanism and guilt was a very European thing, which the Goans seemed to have caught because of long rule by the Portuguese. Perhaps David felt he was caught up in a situation beyond his total control and did what he could to change it; but where he could not change it, he tried not to live by double standards.

Still, George liked the Goans. They were not bad people, and when he went home to visit his family he actually missed the Goans. Such a pity many of them had not become Damibian citizens. Although he had begun to wonder when that strange fellow, Castro Viegas, told him that he had applied for citizenship and nothing had happened. George had had the impression that citizenship had been granted to all non-Damibians who applied for it, unless there was something specific against the individual. Didn't the political leaders periodically accuse East Indians of not accepting the offer of citizenship and sitting on the fence? He was amused by whispers that some of the older Goans had been afraid to speak out against the change of name because they were afraid he, George Kapa, would arrange to have them deported! He disliked the current Minister of Internal Affairs since the time at University when the Minister, then a senior, had taken George's jane away. Since the coup George had stayed as much out of the sight of the Minister as possible. In any case, who would deport such a harmless, useful people as the Goans?

He had reached his driveway. He lived high up on the hill, on an estate just off the road leading to the peak. It was very dark. The area was poorly lighted. It was full of huge cypress trees and elephant grass which sometimes hid breeding grounds for mosquitoes. Useful when he needed mosquitoes for experiments. It was also ideal grounds for *kondos* and his house was burgled twice before the U.N. installed a high barbed-wire fence around the place and hired two armed guards from Secon, for "Security Conscious", a British firm. He identified himself to the guard and drove slowly because of the humps in the road, built to get at drivers like him. With his Peugeot 504, he always felt restless driving under 50 m.p.h.

He parked his car in the garage and entered the house. It was one of these "all-purpose" houses, sort of colourless, classless boxes that the British started building when they knew that their rule in Damibia was coming to an end.

His wife and child were away, visiting her parents. Should he call Gertrude, the ever-willing Gertrude, for some fun? No, lately he had begun to suspect that she had been hired by the regime as an agent. He would look up Janis Cooke, the English secretary who had a passion for black flesh. Independence had actually freed the English – freed them from having to carry the burden of white moral superiority before the black people. Now they could behave as they felt, without restraints – and were they making up for lost time! The White Goddess off her pedestal was nothing but a bitch in perpetual heat. Janis was a good lay, as the Americans would put it, although George often found her rather boring: she did not have any sexual refinement but came at him like a wild animal. He liked to make the first moves, for the woman to respond to him and not make demands of him.

It reminded him of old times, when he used to visit one of his uncles. His uncle was a servant to a very fussy colonial English woman. "Boy! *Laeta chai! Sababu apana fagia jumbani!* Boy!" And with Janis, "George! Punish me! Open my door to paradise with that lovely, large key! Screw me up good and proper!" Janis spoke English and not bad Swahili but she wanted him to "*fagia*" her "*jumbani*". George could not pass up a chance for sexual revenge against the British. Did he not see the white men making merry with African women when he was a child? No, Janis could do. She tended towards the fat side – God, was she fat! Five feet eight inches and 42, 33, 42. No Englishman found her attractive, though an American, with their obsession with bosoms, might have given her a second glance. But George liked his women to be plump. None of that English passion for skin and bones. When he clutched at behinds he like them to be buttocks, not Oxfam posters.

He would clean up first. He had a refreshing shower. None of this English filling of the tub and lying down in it, so that one could see all one's dirt on the water that would stick to the body when one got out. No wonder the British always smelt and had all this obsession with deodorants! He had bought himself a shower attachment. Aaaahhh! It always reminded him of the days he used to swim in the river and get really fresh.

He changed into something light, put on some Brut after-shave lotion – Janis liked Brut, because that is what she wanted George to be – and combed his hair before it dried and became too woolly and stiff. His hair always shrank after a bath. David D'Costa liked to think he was an African but he did not know the real problems of being African!

He turned on the television to listen to the news, although it was past 10 p.m. Thomas Kisirwa came on, with his horn-rimmed glasses and his horn-rimmed Damibian-B.B.C. accent.

"To end the news, here is a summary of the news. His Excellency the General has announced that, in accordance with a dream from God, East Indians have to leave Damibia by the next moon."

6 "All East Indians who are not Damibian citizens must leave the country before the next moon. Those who do not leave will be put into concentration camps. All those East Indians who claim to be citizens of Damibia will have to go to the Immigration Department to have their claims verified."

"Damn!" said David D'Costa. "Here we go again!" He had taken the transistor radio to the bathroom so that he could listen to the news while shaving. His thoughts went back over the past few years. He had not known that trying to be the citizen of the country you were born in was so difficult. When Independence had come to Damibia from British rule early in 1963, he had, in a burst of patriotism, applied for Damibian citizenship. This was well before accusations began to float around of East Indians "sitting on the fence". The Certificate of Citizenship had arrived in due course, reading:

Ref. No, 123
Damibia Citizenship
Citizenship of Registration

This is to certify that David William General D'Costa of P.O. Box 73, Lubele, has been registered as a Citizen of Damibia under section 9 (2) of Chapter III of the Constitution as from the date of this Certificate.
Lubele,   *(Signed) E.F. Devine*
6th day of August, 1963   *Permanent Secretary*
Ministry of Citizenship & Internal Affairs
(Issued on the authority of the Minister of Citizenship & Internal Affairs)

And that, thought David at the time, was that, despite the typograhpical error with his third name, Gerald. No longer was he a British citizen. The British were leaving and handing over to the Damibians and so it was but right that he should become Damibian. There was an accompanying letter with the Certificate of Citizenship saying that he had to renounce his previous nationality before a Magistrate, a Commissioner of Oaths or the British High Commission within three months.

And he had to swear an Oath of Allegiance to the new government within three months, also before a Magistrate or Commissioner of Oaths. There had been no problem, so it seemed.

He went to a local magistrate and renounced his allegiance to the Queen of England. Then he immediately swore his allegiance to the head of state of the new nation, who was the Queen of England. That had struck him as odd, but the ways of the bureaucrats were strange. In any case, under British rule, one had to accept many strange things without question. For instance, he remembered the justification for British rule only a few years earlier was that Africans were incapable of ruling themselves. Then overnight there was a different tune: Africans had always been given training in preparation for Independence. Well, here it was. And he was now a Damibian citizen.

No, he wasn't, as he was to discover in subsequent years. The first problem arose because he had to go almost immediately to England on a postgraduate scholarship, presented by the British government to the Damibian government as an Independence gift. Shortly before going to England, he had gone to Leshona to be the best man at the wedding of Adolf Cardozo, a close friend from university days, and had himself fallen in love with a bridesmaid, Josephine Almeida. They had decided to get married after he had spent some time studying in England, but not too long. All went according to plan, and he returned after two terms to Damibia to marry Josephine.

Josephine had come over from Leshona and they got married at Lubele: a typically big Goan wedding at the Church, with about 800 guests at the reception held at the Institute and with enemies-for-life of those Goans who were not invited. David was to return to England for the third term within a week and there was no time to waste in getting his wife registered as a citizen to make a new passport so that they could make it to England.

He was advised instead to let her travel on her old passport, a British Protected Passport, until they got to England, where they would have all the time to get her registered as a Damibian citizen at the Damibia High Commission. So he went to the British High Commission. The trouble, they said, was that his wife was now married and would have to change her name in the passport. Well, could they do that then? No, because she had a British Protected Passport of a neighbouring country, now Independent. Well, what was the solution? They were willing to make her a new British Protected passport, valid for a few months, to get her into England so that she could then have the time to register as a Damibian citizen.

They had gone to England, to Birmingham. There he wrote to the Damibia High Commission in London to explain the position and apply for Damibian citizenship for his wife. By reply, he was told that the High Commission was sorry but the time-period for non-Africans to apply for automatic citizenship had expired and he would have to wait until he returned to Damibia to apply to the right authorities. Meanwhile, the first child was born, a daughter, Sharon Michelle.

On completion of the postgraduate course on administration, he had to extend his wife's passport and to place his daughter on the passport so they could return to Damibia. All this was done and they left England and arrived at the Lubele airport.

"Your wife and child do not have an Entry Visa into Damibia," said the airport immigration officer.

"But I was studying in England..."

"I am sorry, they will have to return to England by the next fright." He had trouble pronouncing his "l"s.

"But I was sent there by the Damibian Government!"

"I'm sorry, regulations are very crear on this matter."

Fortunately, at that moment, one of the airport employees, Nicky Correa, came over and explained the situation to the man and pleaded with him to let David and his wife and child in. A compromise was finally reached: David would have to pay Shs.100 for a Temporary Visa for his wife and child, valid for two months.

David went to Blanwa, to one of the new five-storeyed buildings, to seek the advice of Mr. Leo Baretto, an old friend of the family. Mr. Baretto had worked as a law clerk and used his knowledge to qualify as a lawyer, going to England in the last stages to sit for his exams and be called to the Bar. After qualifying, he had gone back to his old office, now called the Ministry of Justice; the civil servant instinct went deep in Goans of Damibia. Mr. Baretto told him not to worry, there was no cause for alarm. He picked up the phone and spoke to somebody. Then he said, "Just fill this form and take it over with twenty shillings to Mr. Gozi in the Immigration Department. There is no difficulty. This is only a formality. In the meantime, you can ignore the Temporary Visa. After all, they cannot send your wife and child away from you!"

David filled up the form and took it over to the Immigration Department. After waiting for thirty minutes, he was admitted into the office of Mr. Gozi. In later years, he was to remember that that was the shortest period of time he spent at the Immigration Department waiting to see an official.

Mr. Gozi said, "Oh yes, you are the person Mr. Baretto spoke to me about. Yes, let me check your file. Do you know its number?"

David didn't know the number. "Hmm, that's a problem," said Mr. Gozi. "Anyway, I will take your application and the money. This is only a formality. Under the law, your wife and child are entitled to become citizens. This is an administrative matter."

So David left the matter and went on, like other Goans, to join the Civil Service, being posted to the Ministry of Forestry & Conservation.

Soon, it was time to travel to Leshona to visit his wife's relatives. In the meantime, another baby had been born, a son, Felix Albert. David went along to the Immigration Department to see Mr. Gozi about his application for citizenship for his wife. The office-boy looked at him as though he were a criminal and only after an hour did he tell him that Mr. Gozi had been transferred to another Ministry. Could he see anyone else, inquired David. After another hour, he was admitted into the office of Mr. Labena.

"What is the problem?" asked Mr. Labena.

David explained.

"Well, it is no difficulty. What is your file number?"

David didn't know.

"That will cause some delay." Mr. Labena sent for some files. A huge pile arrived on his desk. He flipped through them.

"I think I have found it. Yee-es. Well, I am sorry. Your wife's application was about to be approved when there was a directive that there should be a general clamp-down on applications for citizenship."

"But my wife's application is a formality," David protested. "I've checked into the law and there should be no difficulty at all. The law says that the wife of a citizen can become one merely by having her name registered and paying the fee."

"I'm sorry. That is the directive."

"What am I to do now? I have an immediate problem. I have been given my leave and am planning on leaving for Leshona. How are we to travel?"

"Let your wife use her old passport."

"But it has expired."

"Get the British to renew it."

He had no choice but to go again to the British High Commission. There, too, he had to wait for a long time. East Indians generally were beginning to be looked on with suspicion by both the Damibian and British authorities. Those who have a common enemy can be friends. The British passport officer agreed to extend the passport for one year if David obtained proof from the Damibian authorities that his wife was not a Damibian citizen. Back he went to see Mr. Labena.

Mr. Labena was quite willing to provide the letter. "Let me look through her passport," he said.

David handed it over.

"Hmm," said Mr. Labena, flipping through the pages. "Do you know that your wife is in this country illegally? She should actually be deported. She does not have a Dependant's Pass or a Special Pass." David began to sweat. "Anyway, it is no problem. I shall stamp a Special Pass on her passport and provide the letter." The Special Pass cost Shs.100 but David was thankful for small mercies.

David was back at the British High Commission. The passport was extended. But then there was the question of the new baby. Children were always put on the passport of the mother. Yes, agreed the British officer, but the second baby was not British. But, protested David, the first child was on the passport.

"Ah, yes," said Mr. Dickens, "but, you see, the first baby was born in England and that makes her British. She is more

British than her mother. She has the right when she grows up to settle in England. But the second child was born in Damibia and so he is a Damibian citizen."

"How then are we to travel to Leshona?"

"Go back to the Damibian authorities and tell them to put the child on your own passport." David went back to the Damibian authorities, who told him that the child could not be put on his passport because the mother was not Damibian and he was a Damibian by registration; therefore the child was not Damibian. David and Josephine had to travel to Leshona with Sharon Michelle and leave Felix Albert with David's mother. After his return, a compromise was worked out with Mr. Dickens. The British were great compromisers, despite their image of living by unchanging laws, and the second child was put on the mother's passport with the proviso that this child was not a British citizen.

The general clamp-down was lifted, but everyone who had applied for citizenship had to apply again, paying a higher fee. The reason for the clamp-down was that the nation had declared itself a republic, with a local Head-of-State. Back to the old routine, David thought. He obtained the forms, filled them, got them signed by a magistrate, and submitted them. Once again, he was told that the whole matter was a formality, there was no problem. No citizenship ever came through.

David's passport had expired. He decided to telephone the Ministry of Citizenship & Internal affairs to find out how to renew the passport: anything not to go in person to the Passport Office and be treated by the office boys as a criminal. He was told to fill in the appropriate form and send it in to the Passport Officer with accompanying payment by registered mail. He did so, and the passport vanished without a trace. When his Ministry decided to send him abroad for a meeting, he was without a document for travelling. He went to the bank and asked for all his cancelled cheques. This included the cheque for the renewal of the passport. Then he went to the Passport Office, taking an official letter from his Ministry that the passport was urgently needed. He was not believed when he said that he had sent in his passport; until he produced the cancelled cheque. After that, he was given the runaround. He was told they would make him a temporary travel document, valid for three months. When it expired, perhaps his passport would be ready. The three months expired, and there was no sign of his passport.

"David, you simple," said Castro Viegas. "I know what going on. Passport sold for one thousand shillings to Indian. There is Ramnik Patel travelling round world on David D'Costa passport."

David had to travel abroad again, this time to Sweden for a meeting. Again, he had to obtain a temporary travel document. At London airport, he was given twenty-four hours to leave, although he was leaving in only three. He was told that when coming back, if he did not want to be deported, he would have to go to the British High Commission in Stockholm and get a British visa.

"This travel document is not proof of citizenship," said the dried-up woman in a dried-up voice. "We have to be careful about the people we let into England. So many stay on and don't leave, you see."

"I have proof that I am a Damibian official," said David, producing a letter he had had the foresight to prepare himself on the Ministry stationery and have signed by his boss.

The woman read the letter. It said, "To whom it may concern: This is to certify that Mr. David William Gerald D'Costa is a Senior Assistant Secretary in the Ministry of Forestry & Conservation. He is attending a meeting at Stockholm, Sweden, on behalf of the Government of Damibia."

"Yes," she said reluctantly, "this is proof that you are an official in the Damibian Government. It is not likely that you would run away from such a high office, is it? I will give you a visa. But the British Immigration officers will have to be convinced that you are honest, that you are only making a brief stop in the country. Fortunately," she laughed in a crackly voice, "you do have an honest face. We British are great judges of character."

And so are you, you dried-up old bitch, thought David. That is why you were able to deceive half the world and rake in its wealth to build up that tiny little lump of shit growing out of the Atlantic. But he didn't say that aloud, not even to the officials at Heathrow airport. They were deceived by his smiling exterior and permitted him to stay on for one week. Damn you, ignorant idiots, thought David, by letting me stay here for one week, you are earning your wages. With the diminishing profits of a diminishing empire, how could you earn your wages if it weren't for foreigners coming in to do menial jobs and other foreigners coming in to buy some of your shoddy products?

The next time David had to go on another official trip, he refused to go with his travel document. He spoke to some of the Secretaries in the Ministry of Overseas Affairs, who arranged for him to see the Senior Passport Officer. The Senior Passport Officer told him to fill in a new form for a new passport and to come back the next day with all the relevant documentation. The next day:

"Where is your Certificate of Renunciation?" asked the Senior Passport Officer.

"What is your Certificate of Renunciation?" asked David.

"The Certificate with which you renounced your former citizenship. Unless you did not renounce it."

"Of course I did," said David. "I remember renouncing my allegiance to the Queen and then immediately swearing it to her again – as head of state of this country. But damn – er, I mean, but that was, um, five years ago. I don't remember what happened to the Certificate. My father died while I was studying in England, on a Damibian government scholarship, and most of his papers were lost. Maybe my Certificate was among them. But I have my Certificate of Damibian citizenship ..."

"Sorry," said the Senior Passport Officer. "The law is the law. You need to produce the Certificate of Renunciation before I am authorized to give you a new passport."

"But what can I do?" wailed David. "I am to leave in three days to represent the government in Ghana! How am I to travel?"

"Tell you what," said the Senior Passport Officer. "You could go and ask the British High Commission whether it has a record of your Certificate of Renunciation on its files. In the meantime, I will give you a temporary travel document, valid for three months."

David went back to the British High Commission. He waited and waited. Many other lost souls, Indians, were also waiting. The British Government had just passed a law requiring all East Indians who were British to apply for vouchers if they wanted to go to their country of citizenship, and only a few thousand were accepted each year. All the Eastern and Central African countries which had been under British rule retaliated at what they considered Britain's high-handed method of landing them with unwanted people: by sacking brown Britons to see what the British would do. The British denied any responsibility it had over these Britons, calling them not "British citizens" but "British passport holders", thus making it seem like they had been done a favour out of the goodness of the collective British heart. David thought wryly that most of the Indians here were Britons only because Damibia had formerly been British; they did not hold passports, as one could judge from many of the people at the High Commission. The passport is an indication of privilege and many of the Indians here were poor. A few Indians, though, would be greeted by smiling British officials and taken in while the mass stayed outside the gates without hope. Could it be that those Indians had bribed the British officials?

David was reluctant to think so. But he wondered whether the British had deliberately provoked the release of so many East Indians on the "market". Britain could pick and choose the ones she needed to prop up her tottering, empire-less economy. She could do this quietly and if the news leaked out she could hide behind a humane image.

David gave up. He returned to his Ministry and phoned from there. He knew that a call from a Ministry always got results. Particularly the Ministry of Forestry & Conservation because it bought so much equipment from Britain. It worked: David spoke to the British Second Secretary, Keith Rake. Mr. Rake told him that he could check through the records. A few minutes later, Mr. Rake told him that they had records for Renunciation by all sorts of D'Costa, including his brother, Evaristo, but none for him.

"Good Dog – er, God, does that mean that I am still British?" shouted David, not thinking of the possibility that he could be dispossessed of Damibian citizenship and denied British citizenship as well.

"Well," said the Oxford-accented Rake, "we will have to check. For 1963, we did not keep records of Renunciations here. We sent the records to the Home Office. I'll write to the Home Office and let you know in five weeks."

"Shall I get in touch with you?" asked David.

"No, that will not be necessary," said Rake. "I'll let you know." David agreed to wait, still intimidated by an Oxford accent.

In Accra, David was informed on the first day of the meeting by his hosts that there had been a kidnapping in Damibia – a high diplomat of the British High Commission had been kidnapped. His name: Keith Rake.

When David returned to Damibia, Keith Rake had been found on an island. A Commission of Inquiry was being held to prove to a disbelieving British Government that Mr. Keith Rake of the Oxford accent had kidnapped himself. It emerged that Mr. Take, as the newspaper called him, had been selling entry vouchers to brown Britons trying to get to Britain and selling British currency on the Damibian black market, for which he was given free trips home by the local Indian travel agents and pocket money to spend at home. The "prosecutors" suggested that Mr. Rake had such a guilty conscience that he was beginning to fear he would be found out by his government. So he decided to kidnap himself, making it appear that disgruntled East Indians had done it. He hoped that when he was eventually rescued, with the British monarch's penchant for knighting Britishers who got into hot spots with unfriendly governments, all doubts would be swept aside and we would probably have a Sir Keith. Maybe Rake had expected something to find the elusive Certificate.

The Commission dragged on for seven weeks. David had to travel again to Europe. This time, he absolutely refused to go without a passport. His friend at the Ministry of Overseas Affairs arranged for him to see the Documentation Officer. The Documentation Officer was very sympathetic and told him that there would be no problem. Within four hours, he had a new

Damibian passport, looking sleeker and less British than the old one.

Now, barely two years and one General later, there was the old situation again. Would there be proof in the mysterious files of the Immigration Department of that talisman, the Certificate of Renunciation? What had happened to it? Had it been printed on self-destructive paper, like those tape-recorders in *Mission Impossible*? And what period was "by the next moon"? He would have to check the calendar.

"Dave! David!!" called out Josephine, startling him out of his reverie. He nicked his chin and had to dab at the blood with a towel. "Are you going to stand there all morning looking at yourself in the mirror? Aren't you going to work?"

David hurried through his shave and sat at the table for breakfast.

He would soon find out.

7 Three days later, while the people were still trying to figure out when the next moon was, guerillas attacked...

Who were the guerillas? Nobody knew. It was suddenly announced over Radio Damibia, "Guerillas have attacked. They have captured Mbaya and Sabada, but nobody should worry, everything is under control."

Next it was announced that the guerillas were from Leshona. The socialist President of Leshona, Oswald Mboye, had said, "We did not fight for Independence only to have it hijacked." He had refused to accept that the General was any people's leader. "I have offered political asylum to the rightful civilian leader of Damibia, President Paul Mbuyiseni."

The non-recognition seemed to drive the General crazy. How dare the very moral Mboye refuse to accept the dictates of God? He ordered his soldiers to attack Leshona and overthrow the regime of this upstart. He was assisted in drawing up plans of invasion by David Michaels, head of the Department of Civil Bureaucracy, and Graham Moore-Diamond, an Englishman who had mysteriously turned up in Damibia one month before the coup.

It was rumored soon after that Moore-Diamond and Michaels had drawn up the twenty-four reasons the General gave over the radio, television and newspaper as his reasons for taking over the government. The General did not read the reasons himself. His English was not good at the time and he had some problems reading his thirty-second announcement of the coup. He had meant to say that he had taken over the Government of Damibia by the Grace of God to "restore democracy and suppress corruption" but, said, instead, that he had done it to "destroy democracy and impress corruption". So the Oxford-trained Kisirwa read the Twenty-Four Reasons that evening, carefully drawn up so that there was something for everybody in the country who felt disgruntled. Meanwhile, the General started attending a crash course in English at the Department of Civil Bureaucracy.

It was no surprise that Moore-Diamond should have been involved in planning the attack on Leshona for he had acquired experience of such matters during the Nigerian Civil War. The attack had taken place and the General's soldiers had been defeated by the police of Leshona. The General's soldiers had only had experience fighting unarmed civilians. "They fought like devils," said one of the Damibian survivors. "They knew that if they did not, they would find themselves ruled by the Devil Himself."

That was not what the Minister of Overseas Affairs, a brother-in-law of the General, said when he returned from a meeting of African Foreign Ministers held at Leshona. President Mboye compromised and modified his hostility to the regime of the General since much of the old administration had survived into the new; he had permitted all representatives of the new regime to attend meetings at Leshona except the General. Besides, this would make it easier for people who wanted to defect. The Overseas Affairs man, Lazarus Gowada, had said that the people of Leshona were fed up with Mboye and wished they had the General instead. So when the guerilla attack began and it was announced that it was Leshona that had attacked, the people of Damibia said that it was the fault of the General: the people of Leshona had wanted him but he had not gone. So they were coming to get him.

The General fell into a blue funk. He could be seen on his Jeep, specially prepared for him in a foreign country so that he could give the impression of being one with the people when he drove around. His Jeep was the closest thing to a tank short of being a tank. He could be seen in his Jeep outside Lubele, six hundred miles from the battlefront, directing operations over shortwave radio. Ronald D'Mello could pick up his battle commands over his radio. The General was only four miles from the airport so that he could fly off if the guerillas won. The General was sure that the guerillas were led by Captain Oma.

The guerillas did not win.

A Central Afrilines plane was found at Njara, a new airport in Leshona close to the border with Damibia, its undercarriage jammed. Nobody was publicly able to explain how it had flown from the main airport of Leshona at Muduku to Njara airport. Ronald found out what had happened when he slept with an airhostess. She told him that a pilot had told her – doubtless when she was sleeping with him – that the Central Afrilines plane had been hijacked at the main airport of Leshona at the start of the guerilla invasion. The guerillas were Damibians in exile, most of whom supported President Mbuyiseni while some only opposed the General. The idea was that a Damibian pilot would fly the plane to the unopened Njara airport near the border, fill it up with fresh guerillas, fly it into the Lubele airport as a regular scheduled flight; and as soon as it had landed, the guerillas would leap out and immobilize the Damibian air force.

By international standards, the air force was small; but even a few MiG-21s and Mirages, discarded by the Soviet Union and France, could do a lot of damage. Once the air force was immobilized, it would not be able to bomb the guerillas attacking by land over the border. But the Damibian pilot was not as good as he thought. He had been demoted several times and had always moved back by presenting a case of racial discrimination. When bringing the plane in to fill it up with guerillas, he forgot to release the brakes and the undercarriage jammed. The result: no guerillas were able to take off, the Damibian air force was not immobilized and took off to bomb the hell out of the other guerillas (as well as a few bystanders).

The next day, the General's soldiers slaughtered hundreds of people in the areas where the guerillas had appeared to be successful, on the grounds that they had helped the guerillas. Many of the killings were done in public as a lesson to the people who survived. The General was able to visit the battlefront a day later in time for the radio, television and newspaper to tell the nation that he had been able to bravely beat back the guerillas, by the Grace of God.

The General had appeared briefly to have doubts about the Grace of God. He appealed to one of the Northern African leaders, General Effendi, for help on the grounds that he was being attacked by the neighbouring state because he was not a Christian. Muslims, he said, were in the majority and were being oppressed by a Christian minority. The Christian Mboye had attacked Damibia to get rid of the General because he was Muslim. General Effendi consented to send his Brother some troops to save him. He also included some troublesome local guerillas who were not content to sit around for the day God would decide to restore their homeland. The help arrived just after the Damibian guerillas had been beaten back.

"The General has decided to expel East Indians and now he has brought in East Indians to help him!" said the people when they saw the foreign troops being transported in Damibian army lorries from the airport. The Arab troops looked just like the East Indians being expelled. What is more, they began to identify more with the people who looked like themselves than with the indigenous Damibians, who were black and, in recent history of Northern Africa, were slaves. The saviours used to sit around in the Damibia International Hotel, drinking on their generous allowances and fraternising with East Indians. When they were sufficiently drunk, they would get up and abuse the first Damibian they saw:

"Hey, slave! Why did God cook you for so long? Why did he not take you out of the oven when you were done just right, like us?"

"Who are these East Indians, acting so arrogant?" said the amazed Damibians. They were used to quiet and docile East Indians. "Aren't they afraid of being taken to Tokyo?"

The people had named the Magende prison "Tokyo" because President Mbuyiseni had been overthrown by the General when he was attending a conference at Tokyo. Hence "Tokyo" – once you went there, you did not return.

To their surprise, the East Indians would say "Take them away!" And the surprised Damibians would find the orders of the East Indians being obeyed by the General's assassination squad.

Things reached a crisis when the saviours started chasing the wives of the Damibian soldiers – rather, the soldiers in the Damibian army, for most of them were not Damibian: they had been brought in from across various borders by the General. Where women were concerned, the foreign soldiers had no objection to fraternizing with black people.

The General faced a revolt by his soldiers. "Send them away," they said, "or we will send you." On cue, there was an uprising in one of the barracks, only beaten back when the barracks were bombed and then razed to the ground with ten bulldozers, flattening all who were in the barracks, the dead, the dying, women and children.

The General arranged to have a presentation ceremony at State House at night. He thanked his Brother General for sending him timely help. "We appreciate greatly this gesture of fraternal solidarity," he said. The lessons at the Department of Civil Administration were showing fruit. "General Effendi has really helped me. When I visited him a year ago, people said, 'Don't go, he will kill you.' But he did not kill me. Instead, he sent me help to stop guerillas killing me. For this, I want to thank him and award him the Order of the Crocodile, First Class. I also award the Medal of Bravery, Second Class, to each and every one of our brothers sitting here." And the foreign soldiers came forward to receive their medals. After that, there was drinking and merrymaking, and at 3 a.m. they were all taken to the airport and put back on their planes. The planes took off to the heroic sound of "It's a Long Way to Tipperary", played by the Damibian Air Force Band.

That night, guerillas shot at the General's car, killing the driver and the two passengers. The dead did not include the General. He had decided at the last moment not to return to the capital in his car but to fly by helicopter.

8 David D'Costa woke up early on Thursday morning to go to the capital, Blanwa, to have his citizenship papers checked.

He had not gone in the first days of the check-in in the hope that something would happen. There were stories of people who had gone early to have their papers verified and had their citizenship taken away. His cousin had her new passport, issued only six weeks earlier, torn up by a very rude officer. The immigration officers were ordinary civil servants, drafted for the purpose of the check-in. One such officer, a colleague of David's, had told him when the check-in began that he had been sent to the Ministry of Citizenship & Internal Affairs by the Permanent Secretary, where he found himself confronted by a raving Minister. "Take it away," he fumed. "Take it away! We cannot let these bloody *Muindis* keep on sucking our blood!"

Of course, the people knew that the Minister was one of the most corrupt people around. He had been a high official in the previous government, and he was known for cashing huge cheques with his own Ministry, which always bounced. He had become a Minister in the new regime and had immediately electrified his country residence. To compensate for this, he had built a chapel in memory of his late father. Perhaps he wanted to turn God into a business partner. The General had opened the chapel, calling on the people of the nation to bear witness to this great, religious God-fearing son of the nation, the Minister of Citizenship. Someone listening to the General's harangue said to his friend, "No wonder the Minister and the General himself fear God: God is the only person whose body they cannot throw into the lake."

David could not put it off forever. Everytime he thought of going to the Immigration Department, his whole body seemed to turn into water. The General had announced that all those who did not have their papers checked by Friday would be declared non-citizens. David decided to go on Wednesday afternoon but his brother had telephoned from Blanwa to say that there was such a long queue they had better try early the following morning. So David and Evaristo set out at 5 a.m. for Blanwa, which was about fifty miles from Lubele. David did not take his wife along because she had never received Damibian citizenship, despite three applications and several interviews. Always he had been told that it was no problem, but nothing happened. Now, he felt it was not a bad thing, after all.

David let out a low whistle of amazement. There already was a long queue of all sorts of East Indians, of all shapes and sizes, stretching as far as the eye could see, disappearing into the mist round the corner. For a moment, he felt like turning back; but what was the alternative? He found a parking spot for the car. He and Evaristo walked over to the end of the queue, which had actually turned the corner. He had not known that there were so many East Indians in the country! What was it that *Ripley's Believe It Or Not* said? If all the Chinese in the world marched four abreast, the line would never end.

He did not know the people around him. The couple behind were talking in Gujarati. So much for the separateness of Goans, David thought. Here, all were "East Indians": industrialists, *dukawallas*, doctors, chemists, teachers, civil servants, mechanics, computer experts, lawyers, bums, printers, travel agents, nurses, to say nothing about the different "tribes": Ismailis, Sikhs, Gujaratis Hindus, Punjabi Hindus, Pakistanis, Bohras, Parsis, Patels, Bengalis, and, of course, Goans. What they shared was the General's blanket accusation that East Indians had been exploiting the country. The Grim Reaper made no distinctions.

"Do you know what happened after the General's announcement? After people knew that it was serious and not a joke?" Someone a few feet ahead was talking. "After the people knew it was real, they came over to my place – I am a chemist, London-qualified – and started buying all my sleeping pills. I am now completely out of stock!"

David saw a well-dressed young Indian, wearing a black blazer, probably of some English university. He must be hoping the Immigration officials would have the traditional colonially-reinforced respect for the British-educated man. Oh God, thought David, to think that in a crisis our only hope of survival is to separate ourselves from our less fortunate brothers! For the American Jew to anglicize his name and reshape his nose. For the American Black to leave his family and pass for White. For the Goan to insist that he is not an Indian. For the Indian to insist he is a college graduate and not a *dukawalla*. Who made such distinctions? Not the masses. They were the ultimate victims. "People cannot sleep," he heard Black Blazer say.

David used to think that Indians were hated in Damibia. He had read several foreign reports that the Damibians had a "fanatical" hatred of East Indians. He knew this was not true. After the announcement, Damibians of all classes came to apologize to him, to weep, to bear gifts. An old, half-blind woman, whom Josephine used to help with old clothes and David by sometimes giving her a lift to the market, came over to give them a bunch of *matoke*, saying that when they left the country the children would never get a chance to eat *matoke* again.

Mrs. Abala, wife of a Permanent Secretary, who used to bring her child to Josephine's little kindergarten, came over to visit and burst out weeping. David and Josephine found themselves consoling a Damibian, who was supposed, according to overseas reports, to be dancing for joy. The General had abused the deep Damibian sense of hospitality. Still, David had assumed that the *dukawallas* were hated. However, the housegirl, Rosa, had said to Josephine in Swahili, "We will really miss the Indian *dukawallas*. When I go into the shop of an Indian and ask to be shown some material, he shows me all the material he has without grumbling. And if I don't buy, he lets me bargain and lowers the price. But if I go into the shop of a Gembe, he takes one look at me and says, 'You are a Muroto, you won't buy anything.' And he refuses to show me anything."

It was Calvary. David was carrying the White Man's burden. Who had brought the Indians to Eastern Africa but the White Man, David thought. Who had exploited India but the White Man, making it necessary for Indians to leave? Who had exploited Goa but the White Man, forcing Goans to wander all over the world without a home? Who had exploited Africa but the White Man? Who had been so subtle as to turn the two exploited non-white groups against each other instead of against the real enemy? Who had left the country with such a complicated set of rules of citizenship but the White Man? Who had decided to disown its responsibility to its own Non-White citizens but the White Man? The devious British, snarled David mentally. No doubt there were some good British people, and some of the British people in Damibia had actually helped the East Indians who were being expelled, but they were few and far between. They were really honorary Coloured people, thought David. Even Jesus, supposed to be the best of the White Men, was not really White: he was from the Middle East, where all the people were coloured at the time.

A tremor swept through the queue, like the tail of a live snake. David looked up. He saw the General driving along slowly in his Jeep, jeering away at the people in the queue! A few East Indians waved out, and the General returned their wave contemptuously. Thus does the snake hypnotise his victim, thought David. The General was an honorary White Man, a leper in the ranks of the Non-White people.

David took out his hanky and wiped his face. The sun was up and it was burning hot. His mother had told him he wiped his face like an African, using broad movements instead of dabbing at it delicately like a Goan. Ahead, he saw women and children moving to the side of the queue and sitting down on the pavement. An African woman was walking along the queue, passing out small glasses of water. When she came to the man in front of David he had a sip and reached automatically into his pocket. She smiled, shook her head, and moved to give David a sip. David gratefully drank from the springs of her generosity. He smiled, trying to express in that smile his knowledge that she had been courageous to show openly that she had not responded to the daily diet of racial hatred prepared by the General.

Did the Damibians hate East Indians? Who spoke for the people? How did they make their thoughts and feelings known? They had no access to the foreign reporters, thought David. Instead, they made their feelings known in other ways. For instance, the people talked about a Sharma in the industrial city of Makende, a hundred and ninety miles away. The people said that Sharma had been in so much despair after the

General's announcement that he had packed his whole family in his car and driven off into the lake. The car and the bodies could not be recovered, although the people could see them because they were in deep, clear water. David was never able to find out if there actually was a Sharma who had committed suicide, but he took the story as a gauge of the feeling of the people.

Then there was the rumour that the people of lgondo, a small town, were afraid because the local Indians practised witchcraft. It was said that when *kondos* had robbed one of the *dukas*, all the *kondos* died mysteriously within a week. The people said that no Damibian in that town would be willing to take over the shops when they were distributed – for fear of witchcraft. The Indian owners, it seemed, came from a village in India noted for witchcraft.

These days, the radio and television played a signature tune in Lowu, the language of the Binda. The General said that this was a song by the Binda, expressing joy at the expulsion of the East Indians. The song embittered many Goans. David had been sceptical. The overthrown President Mbuyiseni was a Binda and there had been a massacre of the Binda after the coup. David could not believe that the Binda would be so in-sensitive as to applaud a cruel action by the man who had been responsible for killing so many of them. He asked George Kapa about it.

George told him that he had asked a Binda friend about it and had been told that the song was a harvest song. "Do you think we are so stupid and inhuman?" the friend had said. "Listen, when the General comes to visit our area, we dance and sing. The General thinks we are singing songs of praise. He gets his television to film us and show his irresistible power to the nation, to show how he has humbled us. But he does not know that we really sing funeral songs when he visits us. We are singing for our sons and daughters, and we are singing for the General himself. His time will come."

David saw new people ahead of him. What had happened to the ones who were there earlier? Were people jumping the queue? Damn it, they were all in the same boat and they had better not rock it to save their own skins. He was passing a hump on the pavement between two showrooms. Someone was sitting on it. He looked familiar.

"It's David, David D'Costa, isn't it?"

"Is that Jules Tavares?"

"Yes, it is."

My God! Was that really him? He had been two years ahead of David in the Lubele Goan Primary School and he was considered to be one of the most brilliant of the students around. His father was one of those rare business Goans: he ran a bar in Kakundu, eighty miles away. When Jules had finished primary school, his father had decided to send him to the coastal town of Mamata at Mozania, which had good secondary schools, so it was said. He had finished with a brilliant Cambridge Overseas School result: a distinction in all subjects except one. This one was English. Under the rules, without even a credit in English, he got a Second Grade. It meant you were a second-grade person, like low-quality eggs. It was said that his father could not live down the disgrace and did not appear in the Goan community for several years.

Without a good result in English you could not get a scholarship to a university abroad or go to the local one, which was only then opening its doors to East Indians. The fact that he knew enough English to obtain distinctions in the other papers did not matter – his Second Grade was the mark of Cain. Every student had known how important it was to know English, to speak and write English the correct way. Most students, including, it appeared, Jules Tavares, had learned English by reading and emulating the great classics, storing away beautiful phrases like monkeys stealing bananas. They did not trust their own inventiveness with the language.

They did not know that in England itself there were a thousand ways to speak and write English. They did not know that if they could go to England the local Englishmen would compliment them on how well they spoke English and not tell them that they had to improve it. They didn't know that the examination papers were not marked by superior Englishmen holding the keys to heaven and hell but by African and Indian students trying to earn some pocket money for their vacations on the continent or next year's board and lodging. Such students would not be impressed by perfect English phrases as they lived with the reality of England, with bad English and slums and racial discrimination. As a Nigerian doctor complained to David in England, "Colonial subjects are the best speakers of textbook English in the world." He was complaining that he could not understand his English patients.

No, the examiners were only going to give high marks to the occasional essay from the thousands that captured their dulled and deafened interest. Moreover, since they had been through the mill themselves, they were not going to have very much patience with people who had not learned the rules of the game. David had. He had read a book called *How to Pass Examinations*, which he had asked his father to order from England. David read that it was the unusual essay that struck the examiner, so he had chosen a common topic for his finals, "The Man I Admire Most", and had written about Elvis Presley. He got a distinction in English.

Jules Tavares had paid the full price for not knowing that it was all a game. He was only able to get admission into the new Teacher Training College, which took rejects by holding out the bait of a scholarship to England when one finished. By the time they did finish, all vague promises had been forgotten and Jules had to teach in an obscure primary school. He lost the nerve to break away and do something daring such as become a travel agent, the new attraction for adventurous young Goans. David had not seen him for years but had heard that he had had a nervous breakdown. My God, he looked it. The thing must have eaten into him, like white ants eating into a tree until all that was left was the shell. This once bright and smartly dressed young man, once held out at the Goan Primary School as a model to all the others, who used to be teased for having ears and dressing like Bing Crosby, was now dressed shabbily, his trousers baggy, his hair uncombed, his shoes unpolished.

"You graduated from university, didn't you? And you studied in England?"

David did not attach any value to these things. His parents had taught him, by word and example, that a human being had a social responsibility to his community and fellowmen. Learning of any kind was to be shared or what use was it? But this was an attitude only one who had degrees could take. The ones who did not have the degrees could only stare at people like him from across a chasm as wide as the Rift Valley. Even the General wanted an honorary Doctorate of Philosophy.

"What do you think will happen if they take our citizenship away?"

David was a high government official and other Goans tended to assume that he was privy to the major decisions taken by the regime. But hell, this particular decision had been taken by God and the General: no other Minister had been in the know!

"Well, let us see," David said. "I don't think things will be so bad. This expulsion order is only a scare. The economy will be in bad shape if there is a mass expulsion. I think the General only wants to frighten those Indians who have started smuggling cocoa to neighbouring countries." When the General had announced his Census of East Indians some months earlier, some Indians had seen the writing on the wall and had, according to rumour, started smuggling cocoa across the border in petrol-tankers.

"You don't have to worry," Jules said. "You have a degree. If anyone is kept on, you will be. If you have to leave, any country will take you." Jules's eyes were darting from David to the front of the queue and then back to David.

"Hey, don't worry, man. You are a teacher, aren't you? Teachers are always needed," said David with a confidence he did not feel.

"But I am only a primary school teacher! And I have two old parents and a sister to look after!" He was practically clinging to David. David's degrees seemed to be a life-belt. David was afraid Jules was going to have another nervous breakdown. Jules's eyes were flicking back and his lips were twitching.

"Primary teachers are particularly needed by developing countries," said David, reading from an invisible World Bank document. "Look, my wife has a little kindergarten at home. When she decided to open it, do you know how many African parents came over to find a place for their kids? Over forty! And my wife had place for only twenty!! One of the parents was so desperate that he even offered to give her a desk if she would accept his child. In spite of the fact that there are already five kindergartens in town! So do you believe for one moment that teachers will be kicked out?"

David thought again of Mrs. Abala. He had met her just after a meeting of the Lubele Parent-Teacher Association. David was a member but had missed the meeting two days ago. Mrs. Abala was such a tough and fearless woman that people said she dominated her otherwise aggressive and loud husband. George Kapa had told David that once when he was drinking at the Lake Hotel in the company of the Abalas and several Permanent Secretaries, Mrs. Abala had said, "Look at this useless man! He went to his woman the other night and then he came and tried to climb into bed onto me. I would have none of it. I kicked the man off. His head struck the wall and he was unconscious for an hour. That should teach him that he cannot play around with me."

"And her husband just sat there like a mouse," said George. People noticed that he had a plaster on his neck. George thought that she was a regular virago. But David always thought that Mrs. Abala looked regal in her wrap-around *kitenge* and head dress. When she drove her Mercedes-Benz, David forgot that he was against elitism and thought the Mercedes-Benz was made for her.

After the P.T.A. meeting, she had told David, burning with anger, that the General and his wives and soldiers were throwing out even Indian teachers because people who had not been to school could not appreciate education. The Minister of Education had pleaded, under pressure from parents, to keep all the East Indian and Goan teachers behind but the General had said "No".

"There is real hunger for education in all of Africa," said David firmly. "Don't you see kids walking several miles to school every day? Even if your citizenship is taken away, which is by no means certain, you will not be asked to leave the country." God, David desperately wanted the queue to move on.

Jules's eyes darted to the front of the queue. Occasional wails could be heard from the front. Someone ahead of David said that an official was moving through the queue and already dispossessing people.

9 "East Indians are reminded that there were thirteen days to leave Damibia!"

Gerry Kern watched Tom Kisirwa on his thirty television sets and decided he had to do something.

Gerry Kern had come to Damibia a few weeks after Independence. He was a New Yorker, of immigrant Polish parents. He was what is known in the business as a hustler. He had learned from experience that he would never make the grade in America with a Polish, un-American, un-Anglo-Saxon name like Josef Kerensky. After all, hadn't Issur Danielovich had to change his name to Kirk Douglas and Daniel Kaminsky to Danny Kaye to make a success of their lives?

Josef Kerensky had tried hustling in New York before he wised up – New York, the very centre of the word. But there were too many other hustlers around and he had gotten nowhere. So he decided to light out for new territory, where his American citizenship would be an advantage. Just then he happened to read in the *New York Daily News* of the Independence of Damibia. He liked it: he had had a very Catholic upbringing and liked religious-sounding names. Besides, he read that the country was green all the year round and had an almost constant temperature, in most parts, of sixty to seventy degrees. He was tired of freezing his ass off in his roachy apartment during winter and roasting it during the ninety-plus of summer. Hell was a New York subway ride in midsummer, where temperatures reached 110°F in those uncooled sardine cans.

"That's the country for me," he decided, changing his name and setting out for cool green pastures.

He arrived in Damibia before the Kennedy assassination. Those were days when Americans could walk tall. Though White, they were not the colonial oppressor. They were the good guys. In fact, as Gerry himself pointed out at cocktail parties he gave the Damibian Ministers, the American showed the way to countries like Damibia in winning Independence from England, oppressive England. He had now come, in a spirit of charity, to share his American experience with his African brothers. Why, he said, given time and assistance, Africa could be as great as America!

One of his plans for making Damibia as great as America impressed the Minister of Public Information, Minister Akoni. This was a plan for introducing television to Damibia. For the purpose, a hospital was closed down – after all, there was the beautiful, big, new hospital donated by the British as an Independence present: "Only returning some of the ill-gotten gains," said Gerry to his Damibian friends.

Gerry did not know anything about television. But growing up and surviving in Brooklyn, with its ghettoes and gang-fights and dirty subway station, he had come to know people who could find an old television broadcasting unit, from a small T.V. station trying desperately to modernize or be swallowed up by one of the giants (it was swallowed up anyway). Gerry got it cheap, but did not feel it necessary to pass on the discount to Damibia. After all, he had his expenses, didn't he? And one per cent of the cut would inform Minister Akoni to watch television quietly. The equipment was installed in the hospital by an American television expert – one of Gerry's old friends from way back, from the time they used to go on rumbles together. These countries were hungry for "experts" so why not give them experts? At expert rates.

Minister Akoni announced in Parliament that, in order to make cheap television sets available to the people, and in order to give the country more employment, no sets would be permitted to be imported from abroad or even from neighbouring countries. They would all be made locally by Damibian Teleservices. Under the directorship of Gerry Kern, Damibian Teleservices would employ local people and television sets would already be produced by Damibians so soon after Independence! Also, to ensure good service, only Teleservices would be permitted to repair or service the television sets.

Ronald D'Mello, working at the Ministry of Public Information, quietly took one of the television sets apart. He found out that it was really Japanese. The only thing Damibian about it was a little plastic flag of the country, attached to one corner, which said "Damibia Television". The set cost four hundred shillings more than in Mozania. That is a hell of a lot of money to pay for a little flag, thought Ronald. "Why not?" said Minister Akoni when questioned in Parliament. "At first, they will be more expensive. We must protect our infant industry until it can stand on its own feet."

Meanwhile, Gerry stood on his own feet, getting fatter all the time and looking more and more like a wide-screen television set. And he stood more firmly after the coup, specially ordering a twenty-five-inch set for the General from Germany. What was the use of being a leader, he told the General when making the presentation, if you could not get the best of the neat little transistor radios or super-big television sets?

And now, when thirty Kisirwas said the Indians had to leave for the sake of the economy of the country, Gerry felt a twinge of patriotism. He called a press conference to say he was going to start the assembly of "People's Radios". They would cost only fifty shillings and would employ all Damibian Africans.

One of Gerry's friends worked in the U.S.I.S. He was talking with one of his Damibian colleagues about the latest Western showing in town, *True Grit,* starring John Wayne. The Damibian said that he liked the name "John Wayne" and thought it suited the actor. The American pointed out that the name "John Wayne" was really a movie name; in reality, he said, the actor's name was something like Marion Morrison. The Damibian laughed disbelievingly. The American said that changes of name were quite common in America: for instance, he said, triumphantly picking up that morning's paper, which had a photo of Gerry and his People's Radio on the front, "Gerry Kern's name used to be Josef Kerensky!" This Damibian mentioned it to someone else, who mentioned it to someone who was an intelligence agent. Hungry to justify his keep and earn a bonus, he went and told the General.

"Kerensky?" bawled the General. When the General had turned against Israelis he had wanted to know how to identify Israeli and Zionist agents. One of his advisers had told him that all names ending with "sky" were Jewish. "Josef Kerensky? That man is a Jew! He is a Zionist agent! Out with him!"

Gerry Kern was deported within twenty-four hours for being a Zionist agent. He returned to New York to read the *New York Daily News* and decide what other country he could take development to and whether he should change his name to, say, Peter Kent.

In Damibia, it was announced that Gerry Kern, a Zionist agent, had planned to import bombs under the pretext of assembling small radios; that he was responsible for doctoring television films of the General's take-over, which showed some happy Israeli army personnel and journalists. The films were shown repeatedly on television because the General wanted to remind the people how he had saved them from dictatorship. It seemed that they were forgetting.

10

"My God," said Al Kamena when he saw Kisirwa announce that there are only thirteen days left. This was the toughest assignment he had been given. How on earth was he still to give the General credibility? Well, his job was not so much to make the General's position credible as to keep saying clever things about all kinds of African leaders so that the people would get confused. When Kofi Lumbula, one of the radical leaders of Africa, was overthrown, he had immediately produced an article on the leader comparing him to a combination of Sun Yat-sen and Genghis Khan. The article was beautifully illustrated, in a journal which had been set up for purposes like this, showing the African leader looking into a series of parallel mirrors and seeing reflections of himself, Genghis Khan and Sun Yat-sen. Al had cleverly woven a web of words around the article, saying that while Lumbula claimed he was a "socialist", actually his policy was one of "national liberalism" which, due to his refusal to take advice from economists and his blind passion for organization, ended up midway between "crypto-fascism and international socialisticization".

"Let the readers figure that out!" Al had chuckled. And while they were doing that, they would have no time to investigate dark rumours of Western involvement, through secret agencies, in the overthrow of Lumbula. Nor would they have the clarity of vision to see what Lumbula did wrong and what he should have done and what he actually did that might have made outsiders want to overthrow him. Al made his article look authentic by sprinkling it liberally with selected, disjointed quotations from the speeches and writings of Lumbula. Africa had a deep traditional respect for learning. Al Kamena was not a Professor of History for nothing.

Soon after the coup by the General, Al Kamena had swung into action, before whispers of foreign involvement could be pursued. He had started out praising the overthrown leader, President Mbuyiseni. This was safe enough as the General himself had been advised to praise his predecessor. It would give the General a good image of peacefulness and legitimacy and would reassure the people who were afraid that coups were always followed by violence.

So Al praised Mbuyiseni for all kinds of reasons. He said Mbuyiseni was a general nationalist, a genuine late-fifties and early-sixties nationalist. Unfortunately, he did not quite trust intellectuals. This was understandable in the days when there was heavy tribalism, for an intellectual's first obligation might be not to the nation as a whole but to his own ethnic group (Al said "ethnic group" to avoid the nasty word "tribe" and give his words the air of great objectivity). Al compared the situation to that of other countries throughout history. He compared it to ancient Greece, to fifteenth-century England, to nineteenth-century pre-Yugoslavia. None of his readers and listeners would have the means to check on his references.

But, he said, time had passed; what the nation now wanted was to be taken into the seventies, with true national loyalties. He said that what was now needed was "liberal-state-capitalism" instead of the "state-crypto-social-neo-fascism" of Mbuyiseni. ("Let them decipher that!" gurgled Al. He had a great sense of humour.) And so, by being totally confused, people would think that the General was the natural successor leader. To emphasize this, Al said that in Africa revolutions would not be carried out by a proletariat, which was too small and powerless, but by a "progressive militariat".

Al Kamena revelled in his image of being "controversial". His publishers had taken to advertising his books by saying, "Kamena's forthcoming controversial book ..." Any time any African writer attacked him, he would point out that throughout history intellectuals had been controversial, viz. Sophocles, Lu Hsun, Malcolm Muggeridge. He did not think that Africa needed conformism. He wanted to break away from habits of thought which were a straightjacket. He did not add that he was only controversial among Africans, and not among Western intellectuals, editors and other agents of the mental process. To them, he was always "brilliant". It was such a pity, he felt, that these same Western personages were not African for they knew so clearly what Africa needed.

Sometimes, Al practised his controversy by performing mental calisthenics, by thinking up the most exciting comparisons and finding ways to yoke them together. For instance, he once summoned historical examples to compare Gandhi to Battista, Jesus Christ to Richard Nixon, and President Mboye to an obscure chemist living in France. He compared the General to Touissant L'Ouverture.

But the damned fellow had gone ahead and decided to expel the East Indians! Basically, Al didn't give a damn. All he cared for was the good life and a good reputation. And he could only have the good life if the economy and habits of the country remained linked with the West. He had no strong objection to the expulsion of East Indians as such; he had been cheated by East Indians when he used to sell cotton as a boy to some Indian middlemen. But the expulsion would not look good to the world and to his Western friends, who would only just have been reading about his support for the General. If he didn't do anything, he would lose his reputation for intellectual brilliance and integrity.

"God dammit!" Al said. "Why was I given such a tough assignment! How could anyone have made any credibility of such a lumbering ox!"

\Only a fool, a simple, brutal, childish fool would not have known that the presence of the East Indians in Damibia was part of the game. To imagine that the colonial rulers would be willing to just hand over Independence! Hah! After all, their entire economies had been built up out of their empires. No, they were far-sighted. Wherever they went, they brought in a buffer, scapegoat middle class, usually from another part of the empire. So when Independence came, the people would be made in a thousand ways to blame these foreign scapegoats as the real cause of continued problems facing the people.

When the price of clothing went up, let the people blame the Indian shopkeeper – the people would not know that the European-owned banks had raised the overdraft charges. When the price paid to cotton and cocoa growers went down, blame the East Indian transport owners: don't let the people know that the European shipping cartel had decided to raise its shipping charges. When the masses were complaining about lack of housing, draw their attention to the very visible East Indians living prominently in good houses – don't tell the people that there are Indians who do not have houses and that Indians occupied only ten thousand houses while there were six million of them who needed homes, and don't tell them that these houses were built mainly by European contractors on local overdrafts.

When the people wanted better transport, draw their attention to the thousands of East Indians who owned the cars the people should have owned, not pointing out that Indians owned fewer than twenty thousand cars, and again, that not all Indians owned cars. At the same time, in a thousand ways, make the East Indians feel that the Damibians envied and hated them, that they had only been protected by the European before Independence and that safety still lay in European arms. Voila! Divide-and-Rule!

All the leaders knew how to play this game – whether they were Africans in Africa, Asians in Asia, West Indians in the West Indies, Romans in ancient Rome, English in the England of the Middle Ages, pre-Yugoslavs in the nineteenth century ... they had to play this game because they could not produce miracles, instant and egalitarian development. Blame the alien middle class but throw out only a few hundreds and keep the rest for continual use. It was like sex, thought Al (he liked to think about sex): you could have sex and still have the means to keep on having sex. But this damned fellow was so simple that he did not realize that it was a game that had to be played with finesse and skill! Instead, he was bull-headed. He actually believed all that stuff about East Indians being the cause of all the trouble and was already saying that the future of Damibia would be bright when the East Indians left. But he was throwing the whole lot out so fast – less than three weeks, which was the general interpretation of the phrase "by the next moon" – that the real puppet-master behind the scenes would stand revealed in all his obscene, phallic nakedness (sexual imagery again).

And what could Al Kamena do? What could he do? If he tried to make a case for East Indians, he could be attacked as anti-Damibian, would be called an apologist for East Indian exploitation, and would squander his remaining credibility with African intellectuals. If he kept quiet he would destroy all his credibility with some liberal Western allies and friends; since Hitler's massacres of the Jews and Western silence while this was taking place, the world would not stand by silently and listen to rationalizations of the collective guilt of a whole people. On the other hand, could he speak to the General? Since the General had started feeling the power surging through his hands, he had stopped listening to advisers. God, it had been a grave miscalculation to believe that a stupid fellow like the General would make the ideal leader because he could be absolutely manipulated by advisers!

Now he arbitrarily listened to the first person who came to see him and acted. When things went wrong, another adviser would turn up with something contradictory and blame the first; a message would go through a barely coded public statement to the assassination squad to come and get the man. They would, according to rumour, throw the first adviser into the boot of the car, take him off somewhere, and chop him into pieces in front of some villagers, throwing his body – or what was left of it – into the lake. For instance, there was the time the General decided to do something about the high price of meat. He told the people that his Cabinet was going to meet the next day and decide to halve the price of meat. The next day, meat disappeared – all butchers would run at a loss if they sold meat at such prices, so they preferred to sell nothing. The adviser, a rather leftist fellow, disappeared shortly before the price of meat was raised to nearly double of what it used to be.

"What shall I do?" thought Al desperately. He played around with all the alliterations and slogans he could conjure up. None of them worked. He considered sneaking out of the country. No, that would not do – it would finish him up forever to have praised the General and then to have run away in a crisis. He would have to find a way of running away with honour.

He would launch a three-pronged attack. He would first cyclostyle a statement condemning the expulsion of the East Indians but obscuring the whole issue by referring to similar expulsions throughout history, such as the expulsion of Arabs from Spain and the expulsion of Indians from Burma – no, the latter example would be too close to the bone; instead, talk of the expulsion of Romans from old England. Then he would make a public statement in the Department of Civil Bureaucracy, where the crowd could be a select one. He could make his criticism so obscure, so full of big words, that it would take the General time to study the tapes and realize that he was being condemned for throwing out the East Indians and not praised. Finally, Al would prepare a very blunt and direct press statement for the media, which he would post at the airport on his way out of the country.

11

David D'Costa had never looked so closely into so many showrooms before. He was walking towards the Immigration Department at the rate of about one yard per hour. Was anyone moving? He could not see as far as the point at which the queue reached the door of the Immigration Department. The queue seemed to disappear into a vastness. All he could see was all sorts of brown people, wearing all kinds of apparel. There were women in cotton dresses, silky saris, little children in jeans, babies in arms ... was he glad that his wife had not been granted citizenship and made to join this never-ending line! Even the sun was moving across the sky quicker than the people on this earth.

He inched past a showroom selling the latest cars from France and Japan, owned by an Indian, Govind Prasani. Prasani had emerged several years ago as an Indian leader. It had been good for business to be a leader of a community. But when the General had said, "All East Indians out!", without distinction, all the self-appointed leaders seemed to vanish into thin air and the Indians were leaderless, like a snake with its head cut off. But who were the "East Indians"? David himself used to resent Indian shopkeepers as much as any African did until he had lived in England and discovered that the English shopkeepers were the same. But all that did not matter now. "The General is a great equalizer!" he had heard someone in front of him say. "I even saw Justice D'Sa in the queue" – the same Justice who had a European wife and lived in the European area of Blanwa, having as little to do with Goans or East Indians as possible.

Now he was moving past Nanda Accessories. It had some of the latest fancy gadgets for those who wanted their cars to be distinctive. Young Indians and Damibians liked to race around with loud horns playing rudimentary tunes, or to have white-walled tyres, etc. Then he was facing Musically Ltd., which sold tape recorders, car cassette-tape-recorders, record players, and other such equipment to make life more comfortable for the privileged. This was the main street and one would not pass by the little *dukas* that attended to the needs of the less privileged.

... Six p.m. and he could not even see the entrance of the Immigration Department! How was he going to make it? His brother left his place and went ahead to find out what was going on. He was back after a few minutes, saying hoarsely, "We'll never make it before the place closes for the night! I think we will have to sleep outside here for the night or we won't make it tomorrow as well! You go and I will keep the family place in the queue."

David went to the home of a cousin in Blanwa to have dinner and a bath. It was too far to return to Lubele. He hoped that Josephine was not worried. No, she was bound to be worried. He had better phone the Lubele Institute and tell someone to take her a message; he did not have a phone. His cousin took him to a neighbour who had a phone and he rang the Institute. After a long time, he heard, "Who speaking?" God, it seemed to be Castro Viegas. Well, he would have to do.

"Viegas," he said, "please tell Marcus to tell my wife that I am delayed in Lubele." He had better not speak too openly because the phones could be tapped. "Tell her not to worry, tell her I will come back tomorrow."

"Aw-kay, will do. Er, who speaking?"

Damn this fellow, David nearly spat into the phone. "This is David D'Costa. Tell Marcus to tell my wife, Josephine D'Costa, that I am all right, that I will return tomorrow."

"Aw-kay, will do."

I hope the message gets to her, thought David grimly as he put the receiver back. Hope JoJo doesn't get scared when Marcus gets home, which he will have to do after the bar closes.

Midnight found David sitting on the ground with his back against the wall of one of the shops while Evaristo took his turn to go to the cousin's place. Although many of the people had gone home, there was still a queue. David began to feel sympathy for all homeless people. He claimed to be a socialist, but there were socialists and socialists and he had never before been in a situation faced by "the oppressed people" he talked about. An hour later, David's brother was back. His bottom feeling like it had turned into concrete, David stood up and walked to two men standing and talking near an old white Peugeot 403.

"I told him to leave the country immediately," the tall one with a shock of silver hair said. "But he wouldn't listen. He was involved with the Mbuyiseni regime. But he stayed on after the coup, saying he had done nothing wrong. After his name was found on that letter carried by that British journalist, he should have left immediately! No, he wanted to protect his property, and perhaps his family. He was seen being taken from his office two days ago by Major Ibrahim."

"Are you talking about Ramesh, the lawyer?" David asked.

"Who else?" said the silver one. "I am Feroze Husseini. You are?"

David introduced himself. David knew the other fellow, Horace D'Souza, a doctor, who always liked to show off. Feroze Husseini said, "I too am an advocate. I was a childhood friend of Ramesh's. We studied law together. Then we parted company. On our return to Damibia he went into politics, and although he got into trouble with the British, he had backed the right horse. The People's Progressive Party came into power and he was sitting pretty. Not only did he have some important jobs but he also had big clients, many of them knowing his pull with the ruling party. But he should have known how dicey politics is."

"But I thought he was one of the few progressive East Indians," said David. "He did not sit on the fence, as the saying goes. I thought he was patriotic. I wished more East Indians and Goans had followed his example instead of depending on 'leaders' like Govind Prasani."

"And do you think Ramesh was any less self-seeking than Govind?" said Husseini contemptuously. "I knew him!"

"I don't know," said David doubtfully.

"Did any East Indians follow him?" said Husseini aggressively. "Did he appeal to any East Indians politically? Ideologically? What did he in fact do but look after his own interests? Which sometimes coincided with the public interest. What ideology did he have? Tell me."

David did not know. In fact, although he had often seen Thakore on television, with his moon-shaped face, sleek hair well brushed back and razor-thin mustache, Thakore had never said what he expected of the nation, how he expected the nation to develop.

"He was even afraid of President Mbuyiseni's very mild socialist measures," said Husseini, "because he could lose all that he had accumulated: his house, his fancy electronic gadgets, his Alfa-Romeo, his large bank balance, etc. And now he has paid a heavy price."

"What happened to him?" David was afraid to hear the answer.

"Major Ibrahim stabbed him, tore out his eyes, and threw his body into the incinerator for secret documents in the President's office. Two hours after his arrest."

David thought he saw Husseini's face shining in the dark. Could he be weeping?

"How do you know?" David asked, hoping that he could say consolingly that Husseini could be wrong.

"There are ways," said Husseini, mysteriously. "There are people in the General's office who will tell you anything for a fee."

Husseini took out his handkerchief and blew his nose. "But at least he was lucky," he continued. "At least he was not chopped alive into pieces in the marketplace, as Ibrahim did with Gregory Mawaswa at Kibumba. And at least he was cremated like a good Hindu."

"But surely – well, why was he killed?" asked David. "Just because the British journalist was carrying a letter from Jack Withers with his name on it? There were other names on that letter as well."

"That, and more," said Husseini. "The General does not trust anyone. Do you remember the time the General was accused of corruption several years ago, when he was a major? Who defended him against charges of embezzlement? Or stealing, for the General did not understand the meaning of 'embezzlement'? Ramesh, of course! The General was as guilty as a vulture, but Ramesh was such a good liar – er, lawyer – so skilled at semantics, that he got him off the hook! Only to get himself onto the hook. The British reporter's letter reminded the General that Ramesh was around, living evidence of the General's corruption while the General was posing as a saviour. As for Ibrahim, this was his chance to get a great sports car. His family were butchers in one of the towns and killing comes easy to him."

"I should imagine that your own situation is slightly uncomfortable if you were friends with Thakore," said Dr. D'Souza at last, puffing on his pipe and looking like a magistrate who had just passed sentence. David thought Dr. D'Souza was not very bright but wanted the Goans around to respect him as a great healer and thinker.

"Oh, we had stopped seeing each other a long time ago. I did not agree with his political stance." Husseini shuffled his feet and rubbed his arms to keep warm. "We used to be socialist radicals in England. If I had to join politics, it would have had to be as a socialist. But there was no socialist party for me to join."

"I thought Islam is inherently anti-socialist," pronounced Dr. D'Souza. "The General is anti-socialist, and he is a believing Muslim. I gather from your name that you also are Muslim."

"The General claims to be Muslim!" said Husseini, bridling. "But his actions are not in keeping with true beliefs of Islam. There is a section – or Surah – in the Q'uran which says that if God had wanted to make all men share the same faith He could have done so, and who is man to try to do what Allah does not do? Religion has nothing to do with it. Yes, I am a Muslim and a socialist. As an East Indian in Africa, I would not have started a socialist party: how could I have started organizing the African masses when I would be alien to their daily lives? And I did not support President Mbuyiseni whole-heartedly, although he had skill as a diplomatic chess player. His socialist policies, when he finally came out with them, were too little, too late; without a strong party to back him, to organize and mobilize the people in support, with all foreign interests against his socialism, of course he had to be overthrown. Surrounded as he was by corrupt Ministers and a weak, self-serving Party elite. Of course, the masses didn't care one bit. That is the point at which these foreign-trained army men become the guardians of Western economic interests."

"But I doubt the man is serving Western interests too well with his sudden expulsion of East Indians and the disruption of the economy," said David.

"The forces of the people cannot be stopped today," said Husseini. "It was soon clear to the Western interests that the General had overplayed his hand in stopping Mbuyiseni's socialist measures, which would have in fact guaranteed their interests while giving the appearance of being radical. So a cheap way for the General to get a radical image would be to throw out the East Indians, blaming them for being exploiters, while not touching Western finance and industrial capital. That was a clever move..."

"Announcing the departure of East Indians by 'the next moon' is the work of a lunatic," said Dr. D'Souza. He laughed at his own cleverness and added, "The word 'lunatic' comes from the Latin 'luna', which means being mentally affected by the moon."

"Rubbish!" said Husseini. "It's a very sneaky move. By the time the people have figured out what 'the next moon' means, they will have to leave. They will have no time to plan anything, to take money out of the country, or to sabotage the factories they have to surrender."

"Nonsense!" said Dr. D'Souza, huffing at having the weight of his medical knowledge dismissed so arbitrarily. "The General is not clever at all. He is a very sick man. He is suffering from some disease..."

"Some disease?" said Husseini, jeering. "Well, I suppose you are not ideologically inclined, like most of the Goans. But tell me – what is the disease?"

"I'm not sure at the moment," said Dr. D'Souza, looking, very profound. "It's one of three things: either some rare disease acquired from eating raw meat, or hypomania, or an advanced case of syphilis. Like George III of England, who thought he was an owl in the last stages."

"Incredible!" said Husseini, shaking his head. "I don't believe it for a moment This expulsion was a very clever move, the clever move of a fascist, a brutal capitalist agent, not of a sick man."

It looked like an argument was going to develop. An argument between a Goan and an East Indian is just what we need now, thought David grimly. "Whatever it is," David said, rather loudly, "we have to be the pall bearers for the dying British Empire. For this task, we'd better get some sleep. Tomorrow will be a long day."

12 It was a long day. Several East Indians had started jumping the queue and David had found himself moving backwards. The Indians and Goans who had slept on the pavement began to shout at anybody who slunk up to the queue and, when he thought nobody was looking, squeezed in. When shouts of "Ay, ay, AY??!" emanated from the ragged line, the policeman standing outside the Immigration Department came over, caught hold of the offending East Indian, and dragged him down to the end of the queue. A few unlucky ones were slapped.

David began to hear what sounded like keening in front of him. God, what was going on? Had somebody collapsed and died from the strain? A tall, blue-suited Damibian was moving through the human river, checking papers, tearing some of them up and telling the people immediately that they were not citizens of Damibia. The family of each person thus dispossessed would burst out in anguish. As the blue man moved towards him, David managed to sidle through the shapeless mass onto the other side and was passed over by the man. David was determined to get into the building and be properly checked. He thought he had earned this right by sleeping outside a building for the first time in his life.

It was after mid-day when David entered the building. He tried to look innocent as he walked through the gaping entrance beyond the suspicious eyes of two soldiers. The soldiers seemed to think that if they were not watchful they would be cheated by these sneaky East Indians. At any sound they lifted their rifles.

David was in. Several mini-queues, bisecting one another, women shouting and children weeping, stifling heat and musty air. Immigration officers at counters looking like prisoners in cells, prisoners ready for execution, hemmed in by spectators in front and armed guards behind.

David joined a queue. After fifteen minutes, the officer went out to lunch and David had to move to another queue. He had lost track of Evaristo.

David was at the counter at last. The black man was sitting hunched up, looking very harassed. He looked up and glared at David, as though David were to blame for his suffering. He wiped his face with a large, grimy handkerchief before turning with a snarl to David. There was a long pause. David could see a tussle taking place in the man's mind between his anger at being made to suffer, his Civil Service politeness, and his awareness of his danger if he said anything the guard behind regarded as stepping out of line.

The man asked David for his file number. By now, David knew his number. The obtaining of the file took half an hour. There was no copy of his Certificate of Renunciation on the family file, although there was another form with David's signature, saying that he renounced his previous citizenship and any other citizenship he may have inadvertently held before becoming a Damibian. David was asked to turn in his Certificate of Citizenship and his passport. Wordlessly, like a sleepwalker, David handed over the piece of paper and his passport.

As David discovered when he was joined by Evaristo, his brother had joined another queue, where he was attended by an old schoolfriend. Evaristo's Renunciation was found on file and his citizenship was confirmed.

It was an unshaven David D'Costa who walked away from the Immigration Department, his brain a beehive. What did it mean to be a stateless person? What would it be like going to a concentration camp? What did it mean not to have a country?

13

Looking out of their window, Abdul Aziz and James Wabinda could see the never-ending queue of Indians. They were having their coffee and scratching their heads. The General was making their job more and more difficult. They were his advisers and had been selected because one of them was of the same religion as the General and the other the same tribe. Unlike the General, both of them had been to high school and university; therefore, unlike the General, neither of them was anxious for Ph.D.s. They had returned from university with their degrees, expecting to receive the same good things and benefits that graduates were receiving while they were in high school. All the prizes had been taken by the early starters! When the General carried out his coup, this was their chance. Both had approached the General through friends, made their appeals, and had been picked to be his advisers in the President's Office, Research Division. They were to collect news items about the General from all the world newspapers, they were to advise him, they were to prepare policy statements for him. For this, they were given what they always wanted: big cars, big houses, big salaries and big allowances, so that they could get all the booze and women they liked.

But the job was not so easy. The General had other advisers. There was that British fellow with the double-barrelled name, Moore-Diamond. He was an old reactionary, imperialist agent and all his advice was meant to be in favour of the West and Western interests, business and political, and to sow the seeds of division among radical and progressive African leaders. Not that Aziz and Wabinda objected to the West; after all, all the things they liked came from there. But they had been to university and had a sense of style; and it was very bad style in Africa today to be openly praising the leadership of South Africa, bringing in White South African soldiers into the country, condemning the more progressive African leaders, and so on. It gave the country a very bad image in the O.A.U. No wonder so many African heads of state had refused to recognize the General's coup for such a long time, though many of them were also Generals who had come into power through the barrel of a gun.

Fortunately, the new Foreign Minister, a relative of one of the General's wives, was also a university graduate and did his best to modify the public pronouncements by the General. When the General had praised Vorster and indicated his willingness to visit South Africa and simultaneously attacked as "prostitutes" those African heads of state who did not want "Dialogue" with South Africa, the Minister of Overseas Affairs explained in the O.A.U. that what the General really meant was that if Vorster was sincere about Dialogue, he should invite fearless and honest African leaders like the General and let them look around freely. As for condemning African leaders, the General was condemning them for being half-hearted in their opposition to South Africa: they should have been preparing for battle, which was true Dialogue. Thus did Lazarus Gowada twist the General's public pronouncements into some sort of progressive shape.

The problem at first was that the General listened to anyone – except members of the former President's tribe, who were periodically killed off – telling him anything. For instance, the Governor of the Central Bank of Damibia had told the General while the Production Minister was out of the country that there was a deficit of 900 million shillings. The General had never heard of such a thing as deficit development financing. He publicly accused the whole Production Ministry of stealing 900 million shillings. The Production Minister was to be arrested on his return and it was only a discreet black minute in primary-school English by Aziz and Wabinda to the General that saved him. Apparently, the Governor had been trying to settle old scores with the Minister. But that Minister was a brave fellow and kept trying to tell the General to stop spending the reserves of the country on all kinds of modern, sophisticated arms.

Shortly after the stealing incident, Aziz and Wabinda entered the Central Bank with the Minister and the General to attend a Cabinet meeting. The General turned to the Minister and growled, "What have you been telling? We have no money? Look at all that money there!"

"Your Excellency, can I explain at the meeting?"

When the Cabinet meeting began, the Minister started giving the General a lecture in elementary economics – and the General raised his arm and slapped him! The Minister managed to remain stony-faced. He was lucky. The slap seemed to have removed for the time being all the violence the General had against him. The Governor of the Bank had shortly afterwards been thrown into what the people called the moving hole – the boot of a car – and had disappeared.

There was that other English adviser, David Michaels. He had told the General soon after the coup to say that God had brought him into power. This would solve the twin questions of how he came into power and what made him legitimate. But as the General had begun to gather the reins of power into his hands, he actually began to believe that stuff about God putting him into power! And as he bloated with power, he listened to nobody before shooting his mouth. For instance, that business about expelling the Israelis. They had been invited into Damibia by President Mbuyiseni several years ago to train the army, when they had a young, egalitarian image in Africa. The image had changed, that's the way the cookie crumbles, but it was bad form to throw them out overnight as the General had done.

And now he had decided to expel the East Indians. It was bad enough that he said that they had to leave "by the next moon" but worse that the order included East Indians who were citizens of Damibia. This was bad for the economy because the Indians included not only small *dukawallas* but also industrialists, civil servants, doctors, teachers, university lecturers, lawyers, computer experts, technicians, most of whom had been trained at the cost of Damibia. Even worse, it was bad for the image. Left to his own mental devices, it seemed that the General's policy was two-fold: send people out or send them under.

"First, we must come out with some ideology to explain the expulsion order," said Aziz. "The appearance of God in a dream is not convincing enough. I wonder how he had that dream?"

"Yeh," said Wabinda softly, not sure that the office was not bugged. "Maybe he had that dream because the papers were full of the shuttle cocking of British East Indians who landed in England without entry visas. You remember, the British East Indian family that left Damibia and was not allowed to land in England? They had to keep on flying all over the world. You know the General's love for the Queen. He must have thought that if Her Majesty did not want them, they must really be bad."

"That's not our problem now," said Aziz. "We must first think of some catchy phrase, like that Al Kamena is so good at."

"The General is a military man and we have an economic problem," said Wabinda. "Let us combine the two – some kind of war about the economy."

"That's it!" said Aziz. "Let's say that the General has declared an Economic War. Let's say that the expulsion of the Israelis was Phase I and the expulsion of East Indians is Phase II."

"Hey, good! That sounds pretty leftist, without sounding Communist," said Wabinda. "But let's add some further explanation about the East Indians. Let's keep on saying all East Indians in Damibia are non-citizen businessmen. Remember someone said that if you repeated a lie long enough people would believe it?"

"Hitler!" said Aziz.

"What?" said Wabinda, looking over his shoulder.

"Hitler said it!" said Aziz.

"Okay, okay," said Wabinda testily. He felt jumpy these days. "Then we need some blanket accusation, which people will accept without question just because it is so large and wild."

"Let's use some of the words the General likes," said Aziz.

"He likes some of those big words they have been teaching him in his English classes at the Department of Civil Bureaucracy," said Wabinda. He did not like that other Englishman, David Michaels. He too used to fill the General's head with reactionary ideas. Well not ideas, because the General was incapable of an idea, but with phrases.

"Truth, efficiency, corruption, sabotage."

"Sabotage is fine!" said Wabinda, pleased. "It has a nice sinister ring to it. Let the General accuse the East Indians of 'sabotaging the economy of Damibia'. That will be good for the image, and will get us the support of the O.A.U. and all progressive people in the Third World."

"Right!" said Aziz, taking notes for another "A Spokesman from the President's Office Says" press release.

"Meanwhile," continued Wabinda, "we will have to try and find a way of exempting most of the East Indians that we need so that the economy does not collapse. Such that after the full moon we say that the expulsion is successful and yet we still have the Indians we want. Perhaps we should approach the Minister of Overseas Affairs. He still has the ear of the General."

"Yes, and one day, maybe, the General will have his ear and eye and nose..." Aziz saw Wabinda glaring at him and stopped.

"We could suggest to the Overseas Affairs Minister that the General grant exemptions as a humane gesture. Thus the General will have the image of being a tough, militaristic, no-nonsense African nationalist as well as a humane, non-racist, benevolent father of the nation. This is what we'll have to tell the Minister, and soon. Today. There is no time to waste. Point out to the Minister that the General likes publicity and this will give him a lot of it."

"Okay," said Aziz, opening some of the new mail that had come in. "I'll go as soon as I've finished this. Hey, look at this! This is a gem!" He was looking at a British Sunday paper carrying an account of the expulsion of East Indians from Damibia. The article carried a big photo of the General. The photo had been taken when the General had gone to England to lunch with the Queen in the first heady days of the coup: he had been photographed with the Prime Minister of England but the Prime Minister had been cut out. "He is Nuts!" screamed the headlines of the paper.

"Beautiful, just beautiful!" said Wabinda. His day was brightening. "That will fetch us at least," he said, looking over his shoulder and dropping his voice, "twenty shillings each!"

Wabinda and Aziz periodically found themselves short of spare cash. What they did was they xeroxed several copies of the juicy foreign articles about the General. They would pass copies on to some of their relatives who would go round discreetly selling them. It seems the people did not believe what was said in the local, government-controlled newspaper and were willing to pay any amount for foreign reports about the General and the country. Since all foreign papers had been banned on the advice of Wabinda and Aziz, except for copies coming into the President's Research Division, Wabinda and Aziz soon had a roaring trade going. Who said that only East Indians were enterprising!

14 David plodded up the steps of his house and knocked on the door with a "ta-ta-ta-ta-ta-(pause) ta-ta". He had stopped using his key after the General's announcement while Josephine was at home because it made her jumpy.

"What happened?" said Josephine, opening the door so suddenly that David nearly fell in. She tried to embrace him but he gently pushed her away. He was too dirty and unshaven.

"They took away my citizenship," said David wearily, removing his coat and flinging it onto a chair.

"I was so worried!" said Josephine, trailing David to the toilet. She stood out as David went in and shut the door. "I thought something terrible had happened when you did not return by 8 p.m. I knew the Immigration Department couldn't be open so late. I jumped out of my skin when I heard a knock on the door at 11 p.m. It was Marcus. He did not have much to tell me. He only said that a phone call had come from Blanwa from you, that you wanted me to know that you were all right. But he could not tell me anything more. He said that that crazy fellow Castro Viegas had picked up the phone and he was so drunk that he could not tell him what you said."

David pulled the flush and dragged his feet to the bathroom, Josephine trailing him.

"I couldn't sleep," said Josephine. "I had to bring Snoopy into the house." Normally, they kept the dog out of the house because he was big and liked to charge all over the place. "Every sound nearly gave me a heart attack. I could hear shooting."

David started to brush his teeth.

"I put the children on my bed. I must have fallen asleep at 5 a.m."

David had started lathering his face.

"What happened? What took you so long?"

"There was a very big queue," said David, starting to shave. "We had to sleep outside the Immigration Office!"

"Poor David!" crooned Josephine, putting her arm round his waist.

"They took away my citizenship."

"I expected that!" said Josephine. She was not surprised. "Have you eaten lunch?"

David shook his head numbly.

Josephine gave a start. "Breakfast?" she almost whispered.

David shook his head again.

"They took away my citizenship," said David, washing his face.

"I expected that!" said Josephine, moving to the kitchen to warm some lunch. The cook and the housegirl had gone off for the day. "You were too nationalistic! Couldn't you see that Indians and Goans are not wanted?"

"I'm too tired to argue," said David, going to the fridge and taking out a bottle of beer. "East Indians and Goans are not hated as such. It is a political problem, going back to and created by the British colonialists." David poured the beer into a mug and took a long drink. "The General is a brute!" Then David remembered that he had not put on some after-shave lotion. He went to the bathroom and splashed on some Old Spice Lime. He had bought it because Josephine liked the tang of lime. He moved back to his beer, took another gulp and sat at the table.

"Whether you're right or wrong, we now have to leave," said Josephine, setting the lunch before David. "I told you a long time ago that we should leave."

"We've been through that time after time," said David, taking his first mouthful. "This is my country. I don't want to leave."

"But we have to leave now!" said Josephine. "How can you still insist on staying on? We are forced to leave!"

"I'm not too sure about that," said David. "After I lost my citizenship I went over to see Benjamin at the Ministry of Justice. Remember Benjamin Gwalu?"

"The tubby, easy-going fellow who had lunch with us about six months ago?"

"That's right. He told me that the General had just decided to formally exempt certain people from leaving. Ben has to draft the new law. He said that I am bound to be exempted if I apply through the Ministry. He said that later, when the whole situation has died down, I can apply to get my citizenship back."

"It is not only the situation that will have died down – we too will be dead!" said Josephine. "I cannot understand you, David. The Damibians do not want you. Why do you still want to stay?"

"That's not true!" said David, finishing his beer and opening another. He pushed away his plate, leaving the rice and curry half-eaten. "How many Damibians have you come across who hate us? What about the woman who gave us that bunch of *matoke*? If this were Europe, with the inflammatory statements made by the leader we would all have been massacred by the people. That proves the people do not hate East Indians and Goans."

"But the General does not want us!" said Josephine, clearing the table.

"Who is the General?" scoffed David. "He was not elected by the people. He was put into power by the imperialists, wanting to preserve their interests. He just got out of hand and bit the hand that fed him."

"The General is the man in power and the man with the guns," said Josephine, bringing David a slice of paw-paw. "It does not matter if the people want us. In any case, some of the people must support him or he could not have remained in power."

"Yes, a handful of local people, but mainly mercenaries, soldiers from other countries. What few Damibian soldiers there are, are kept away from the arms. Still, there have been numerous attempted uprisings and assassination attempts and one day..."

"But when?" said Josephine desperately. "The General does not want us, and he has the guns, tanks and concentration camps to finish us off!"

"Nonsense!" said David. "All that business about putting East Indians into concentration camps is all blah, part of the General's military psychological tactics to frighten East Indians into leaving. If they think the General is going to kill them, they will leave voluntarily. But the General isn't going to kill them."

"How do you know? Hasn't the General killed many of his own people already? One moment you say he is stupid, the next that he is clever enough to plan psychological terror tactics! Hasn't he killed his own Supreme Court Justice? And what will stop him killing a few thousand Indians – and Goans?"

"The world will not stand for it," said David, lighting up a cigarette and looking out of the window at the distant blue of the lake. He noticed that the bunch of bananas on the tree was nearly ripe for the picking. He would have to tell the cook to get it off before it was stolen. He had once tried to cut down a bunch but he did not have the skill and made a mess of the stalks. It would make a nice Christmas present for the family and friends. "The world will not stand for it. Not after the killing of the Jews by Hitler."

"Who will stop him?" persisted Josephine. "India? How many millions don't die in India of starvation? And has India shown any interest in the plight of Indians being expelled from Damibia? It is only interested in pointing out to Britain that British Indians are the responsibility of Britain. Which is true enough, but the East Indians and Goans are being turned into soccer balls, to be kicked wherever the players want. Pakistan? How many people haven't just been killed and raped in East Pakistan by their own nationals? Britain? Hah, Britain! She has made it clear she does not even want people of her own citizenship! You are dreaming, as usual!"

"Talking about dreaming," said David, sitting up with a gleam in his eye, "where are the kids?"

"Sharon has gone out to play with her friends," said Josephine, "and Felix is asleep."

"I spent last night being fucked by the Ministry of Citizenship and Internal Affairs," said David. His hand had left the beer mug and was curving around her buttocks.

"Not at three in the afternoon!" protested Josephine, identifying the smile on David's face, like a cat about to have a saucer of milk. "Not just after lunch. We must talk this over. We can't stay on here with one daughter..."

"Blackmail, huh?" said David, getting up to draw the curtains and make sure the door was locked.

"You cannot sacrifice us to your ideals," began Josephine, finding herself being steered to the bedroom and the door locked. "This is a serious matter, and the Canadians have come to the country to take any East Indians to their country..." She found her skirt being taken off by David.

"Jojo," said David, "things are going to get tougher, and you had better get it from me while I still have it. In days to come, I may not be very potent."

Josephine was naked on the bed, but held her thighs together. Unlike most Goan women, she did not have thin legs and thighs. "We must talk it over first. Kisirwa, the newsreader announced this morning, says that we have eight days to leave."

"Cuntmail!" said David, separating her thighs. He entered her, taking refuge from the world of citizenship papers and passports and queues, concerned now with only one kind of internal affairs.

15

"KONDO, SPY KICKED OUT!!" The newspaper had one of the biggest headlines Castro Viegas had ever seen. He picked it up. It was an old paper that had been used to wrap some grapefruit the hotel had purchased from the market.

Castro seldom read the paper. He had some difficulty with English. He read the article, slowly.

Alan Mansfield, a British reporter, was searched at the airport on Tuesday when attempting to leave the country. He was found to have in his possession a stolen copy of the Damibian Book of Residential Addresses.

He was taken to court immediately. He pleaded guilty to a charge of having stolen the book.

Castro shook his head. This English was such a bitch language that he actually thought he read that a man had been found guilty of stealing a Book of Residential Addresses, which one could buy for two shillings from any Post Office or bookshop!

Mr. Mansfield, who works for the British paper, *The Onlooker*, was fined one thousand shillings. Justice Mwala told him at the sentencing, "When the British Christians came here, they taught us not to steal, and you have disgraced the lesson of your forefathers!" Justice Mwala ordered him to be deported as soon as it was ensured that he did not have any debts in the country.

Funny, thought Viegas. The man was leaving at the airport and they stopped him. Now they say they are deporting him. Castro heard the whine of a jet, sounding rather low. He went out through the back of the hotel. The airport was only a mile from the hotel. There was the plane, banking steeply after take-off and climbing north. It was a hard climb over the blue lake and green islands. The sky was clear; maybe the pilot was trying to impress those two White women roasting their flesh near the pool. Air hostesses, maybe, taking a rest before their next flight. That would be a shock for them if the engines got too hot because of the climb. The plane would dive into the lake, like the women dived into the pool! Maybe that reporter was on the plane.

Viegas returned to the paper. There were two more paragraphs.

A letter was found on Mr. Mansfield. It was from Jack Withers, the well-known journalist on African Affairs.

It said: "When in Damibia, contact the following people: Al Kamena, the brilliant historian; Dennis Amadi, Minister of Education; Charles Majangwa, chairman of the leading state corporation; David Michaels, chairman of the Department of Civil Bureaucracy; and Ramesh Thakore, a well-known lawyer and leader of the East Indian community."

The only name Viegas knew was the last, Ramesh Thakore. Thakore often appeared on television. Any prominent East Indian politician would catch one's notice. In fact, Viegas thought that one day he would visit Thakore and seek his help over immigration matters. But he decided to let sleeping dogs lie.

Castro Viegas had come into the country illegally. He had been declared an unwanted immigrant in the neighbouring country, so he had come by bus into this country. He looked like an Arab, what with his dark skin and beard. He had purposely worn a tarboosh. There were Arabs in Eastern and Central Africa from the days of the slave trade and nobody asked for their passports when they crossed the borders.

Almost all his life Viegas was an illegal immigrant, from the time he decided to leave Goa and make a living somewhere. He could cook, and cooks were always needed, on ships, exclusive clubs and hotels. He had learned English by himself but knew he spoke it like he spoke Portuguese. It was good people could not understand him clearly; he never told anybody the truth about himself. For instance, that stupid cook, that Fernandes, was always trying to make trouble for him. No Goan wanted another to succeed! But by behaving strangely he scared Fernandes off. After he had picked up the meat knife and advanced on Fernandes he had been left in peace.

Viegas felt thirsty and decided to go to his room for refreshments. In the evening, he could go to the Institute and ask David D'Costa or Ronald D'Mello about the British reporter.

16

Castro Viegas entered the Institute bar. He heard David D'Costa and Joe Pereira talking as they sat at the counter with their drinks.

"And Ramesh Thakore was done in all because his name was on that blasted letter carried by that blasted British reporter!" said David.

"Those idiots!" said Joe. "The British are all saying that there is no law and order in this country. Then a British reporter comes in, carrying a fucking letter with all those names, behaving as though there is law and order! Stupid!"

"Why British reporter come?" asked Castro, gulping down his beer. He ordered another beer and brandy. He had just seen one of the Greek visitors to the hotel mixing a tort of brandy with each mug of beer. He decided to try the same.

"Well," said David. "You know that *The Onlooker* has been writing a lot of articles on this country, documenting all – or most – of the killings. No doubt the General would not like people outside to know that people are being killed. No doubt he imagines that all these disappearances will be accepted for what he says they are, people running away. So it seems that he got mad at the reporter for *The Onlooker*, Cecil Greaves, who is based in Leshona. He sent an invitation to Greaves to come into Damibia and see the truth for himself instead of writing lies. The General is a great believer in the truth. Greaves knew what kind of truth the General had in mind when he was promised safe passage. Instead of Greaves, it appears, *The Onlooker* sent in a new man, Alan Mansfield. Mansfield was arrested because of the General's frustration that the wrong man had come in."

"And Ramesh Thakore?" asked Viegas.

"Killed."

"Killed? How?"

"He was apparently stabbed, his eyes gouged out, and his body was thrown into an incinerator."

"What is an in-sin-er-er-er–"

"A kind of oven, with great heat, enough to roast meat in five minutes," said Joe.

"You mean, he burnt?"

"Yes."

Castro downed his beer in one gulp. It was laced with the brandy. He fell off his stool and folded into a heap.

"Goddamit!" said Joe, banging his fist onto the bar counter. "Why does this fellow always collapse when he comes to this Institute? We'll have to take him home. He usually lasts longer than this."

"Let's put him aside," said David, "until it's time to go. I'll give him a lift to his place, if you will help."

Joe and David lifted Viegas from the floor. He felt like a string of macaroni. They carried him to the ping-pong table and heaved him onto it.

The next day, Castro Viegas sent some tins of canned meat and a bottle of brandy to Joe and David with one of the Lake Hotel waiters. Then Castro Viegas vanished, as though he had walked into the lake. Nobody knew what had happened to him. A few wondered if he had "disappeared".

Viegas had decided that Damibia was not a safe place to live in. He put on his tarboosh and caught the lake steamer plying the lake between the four countries in Central Africa. Maybe Goa was not such a bad place after all.

17 "My citizenship was taken away because they could not find my file in the Immigration Department," said Joe Pereira, sipping his beer and waiting for the next round of Tombola to begin. "But I have been exempted and am not leaving the country."

It was Sunday morning, ten days after the General had made his announcement of the expulsion. Thomas Kisirwa said in the news that morning that one week was left for the East Indians to leave. The Lubele Institute was having its last big get-together at which souvenir ashtrays with reliefs of wild animals would be presented as farewell presents. There was no time for the normal big farewell party for each individual member leaving. It was a day occasion because it was not quite safe to have a night affair and attract the attention of roving bands of soldiers.

"Good for you," said Dr. Horace D'Souza, looking through the large windows at the bus transporting East Indians up the main road from Blanwa to the airport. Dr. D'Souza was a member of the Blanwa Goan Institute, but it had been seized by the military five days ago and turned into an officers' mess. All members of the Blanwa Goan Institute had been invited to Lubele for this last big function. "As for me," Dr. D'Souza continued, "I am most certainly going to leave before the week runs out, although I was one of the few to have my Damibian citizenship confirmed. The Immigration Officer was a decent fellow; besides, I had cured his wife six months ago."

"Why?" asked Joe, thinking that Dr. D'Souza looked most odd. His head was like a pyramid turned upside down, Wide at the top and tapering to a very pointed chin, like Dr. Sivana in those old Captain Marvel comics.

"Because she was suffering from ulcers."

"I mean, why are you leaving?"

"The General is suffering from hypomania," said Dr. D'Souza, looking very authoritative.

"What's that?" asked Joe, waiting for the Tombola prizes to be announced. Tombola was a lower-keyed, more genteel version of Bingo and Joe had enjoyed himself going to the Bingo halls when he was in England on a seminar. But he had exhausted his passion for the game and had not bought a ticket for the next round. Still, he liked to see the Goans playing Tombola, trying to suppress their greed under the usual Goan social behaviour. Maybe Goans liked Tombola because they believed in luck. They had no choice but to do so since they didn't seem to control their *nosib* or destiny.

"Well, of course it's a nervous disorder," said Dr. D'Souza, sounding as though he had put on his white gown and stethoscope. "But the person suffering from it thinks he is in perfect health. The only thing is that he feels he wants to do so much and there isn't time enough."

Dr. D'Souza had to pause frequently because of the growl of cars coming in from Blanwa and rushing up the hill. Occasionally, they would hear a growing, booming rumble, like an avalanche or earthquake: this would metamorphose into a petrol tanker and trailer charging down the hill after delivering its supplies of aviation fuel to the airport. Petrol was brought to Blanwa by rail from the coast of Mozania and then had to be taken by road to the airport. The booming sound was caused by multiple echoes against the parallel houses of the civil servants. "... so the first thing he tries to do is to go directly to his goal, regardless of the price to be paid or the suffering to be inflicted, regardless of..."

Joe was getting impatient with the litany, the result no doubt of Dr. D'Souza's grounding in Portuguese. The would-be Goan elite took pains in Goa to learn Portuguese and it made their English very turgid and flowery. "They are about to start," interrupted Joe, pointing to the stage, where Ronald D'Mello had just counted the money from the sale of Tombola tickets and had picked up the cloth bag containing the numbers from which the lucky ones would be picked.

"Look," said Dr. D'Souza, "I know the General is suffering from hypomania because Dr. Kaparo, my colleague, told me so." Joe found it interesting how, most of the time, the Goans and Indians had not believed Damibians, but now, during this crisis, they hung on to the words spoken by Damibians as though all of them were gifted with the power of insight instead of being as bewildered as anyone else. It had become the rule not to believe anything said only by an East Indian or Goan and so Dr. D'Souza was trying to convince Joe by quoting authority: a Damibian doctor.

Ronald put his hand in the bag and picked up a number. "All by itself, number one," he called out. Immediately, a lady's voice rang out, "Shake it up!"

"What I'm saying is this – the General has announced that God told him in a dream to expel all East Indians. This means that the General will expel all East Indians, by hook or crook, by whatever means and at whatever cost to the economy. He will kick out those who are not citizens, take away citizenship, use the threat of concentration camps, use the threat of murder, and actually commit murder, until within a very short time, there will be no East Indians left in Damibia. And ..." sweeping his hand around the hall "...no Goans."

Joe gulped as Ronald shook his bag of numbers, saying, "Here we go! I'm shaking for the pleasure of the ladies!"

"But I am exempted," protested Joe.

"Ah yes," said Dr. D'Souza. "Some of the General's Ministers and advisers were wise and prevailed on him to keep behind some East Indians essential to the economy. But they will fall into disfavour at some point and the General will cancel the exemptions. What will you do after the Deadline, only a week away, when there are no countries and no U.N. to take you out and your exemption is cancelled with twenty-four hours notice?"

"Five and four, fifty-four!" called Ronald, looking at the number he had taken out of the bag. "I'll repeat that – five – and – four, fifty-four! And the first number out of the pussy – er, kitty – was an upright number one."

Ronald knew that some of the ladies like his raunchy style of announcing Tombola. Some of the people who had the numbers on their tickets cancelled them with pencils and punched holes in them with burnt-out matchsticks while Ronald passed the numbers to one of the kids to hang on a board containing hooks numbered from one to ninety.

"Are ... are you sure?" said Joe, thinking how much more like Dr. Sivana Dr. D'Souza was becoming. Next, he would be cackling in a high-pitched voice as he threw the switch that would destroy Joe.

"Positive!" said Dr. D'Souza. "Look – another symptom of hypomania. The person feels that there isn't enough time ..."

"Two and seven, twenty-seven!" called Ronald.

"... so he does things earlier and earlier in the day. Notice how the General keeps saying that there is no time to waste."

"Chinese puzzle, sixty-nine!"

"And did you notice how he called up a meeting of the Cabinet at 6 a.m, last week?"

"That's right," said Joe. "The Ministers now have to carry transistor radios with them ..."

"Top of the house, nine and zero, ninety!"

"... or else they won't know when there is a Cabinet meeting on. If they miss one..."

"Two little ducklings, twenty-two!"

"... they would be killed."

"Mark my words," said Dr. D'Souza, "the General's meetings will get earlier and earlier in the day."

"Two fat ladies, eight and eight, eighty-eight!"

People called out "Sena", who was the fattest person around.

"And before it gets to midnight, I shall be out of the country."

"Lucky for some, one and three, thirteen!"

Gerson Mendonca's wife shrieked, "House!" and swept up to the stage to have her ticket checked and claim her prize.

After checking the ticket, Ronald announced, "You are reminded that this young lady left her seat in less than twenty-one numbers!" This was in imitation of Thomas Kisirwa, who from only a week ago had rudely started reminding people after each news broadcast how many days East Indians had to leave the country. This was a sour note. The ladies did not find it funny. Mrs. Mendonca almost scowled as she received her prize.

"Have a drink," said Joe to Dr. D'Souza.

"Yes," nodded Dr. D'Souza. "We might as well drink it all up before they take over all our Institutes."

They both disappeared into the bar.

18

Jacob Britto was one of the fixtures of Lubele. As far back as one could remember, he was at Lubele, like that tall eucalyptus tree at the botanical garden, and just as lined. He lived on the fringe of Goan society. He made very rare appearances at the Institute, and when he did he was always shabbily but cleanly dressed, always wearing his wide-brimmed felt hat like an old-time American detective, like the lieutenant in the Perry Mason television films. But he always paid his Institute fees on time.

Jacob had seen better days. David and Ronald remembered that when they were children and none of the Lubele Goans had cars, Jacob had first one lorry and then two. He was in the transport business and had money to throw around. And did he throw it around! Mainly on Damibian women, with whom he was not ashamed to be seen, unlike some of the other men, who only sneaked around with Damibian women after dark. There had been the scandalous case when one of the respected members of the community had been caught in the house of an *ayah* by her man, with his pants down, figuratively and literally. He was lucky to escape with just a beating, but the story was that his manhood was not so manly for over a month. But Jacob went around openly with his women. None of the Goans dared say anything to him openly because they needed his lorry. Besides, he did not marry and was not betraying any wife left at home to look after the children while he went gallivanting.

As time had gone by, young and dashing Britto had become old Jacob and he had fallen onto bad times. His lorries had vanished. All he had left now was an old Bedford van from the late fifties, which the manufacturers had stopped producing. He carried African passengers locally to the ferry on the lake, transported furniture for the Lubele Institute and did other small odd-jobs. It was a wonder that the van ran at all. Everybody said that it ran on soul power – Jacob's soul. The day it stopped, Jacob would be dead. He did not have the money to replace it.

Many people, Goans, Indians and Damibians, tried to help him by giving him transportation jobs and then trying to pay him double the hiring fee. Once, he had transported a kennel for David D'Costa for five shillings. David had folded the note over while giving it to him. When Jacob realized that it was ten shillings, he reversed all the way to David's house to return five shillings change. He had his dignity and nobody was going to take it away with charity.

Jacob had come to the Institute for the farewell party.

David was looking through the latest issue of *The Onlooker*, which contained news about the expulsion of East Indians from Damibia. The article talked about the property of the East Indians that would be left behind.

"My citizenship was taken away. I received this notice yesterday morning."

Although David had already seen such notices, he accepted the crumpled paper Jacob took out of a rumpled coat. David read it:

MINISTRY OF CITIZENSHIP & INTERNAL AFFAIRS
December 12, 1971

To Jacob Britto, P.O. Box 4, Lubele
Dear Mr. Britto
Kindly remove yourself from Damibia by the 21st December, 1971.
Failure to take the above action may lead to severe penalties.
I am, Sir,

Your obedient servant
(Signed)
F. Nzeogwu
for Permanent Secretary,
Ministry of Citizenship & Internal Affairs

David felt a twinge of bitterness welling up in him. For choosing to become a Damibian citizen instead of something else, an option not open to indigenous Damibians, not only was Jacob being asked to leave with no country to go to but also he was being given less than one week's notice, considering the postal delay. Those who had refused to become citizens had time and countries. What consolation could he offer Jacob? Even this knife stabbing him in the back was written with the formal politeness bequeathed by the British Empire. Maybe the British hangman bowed to his victim before pulling the cord tight.

"Have you been to the Canadian authorities?" David asked. "They have been in Blanwa from four days ago. They have lowered their entrance requirements to accept as many East Indians and Goans from Damibia as possible."

"No," said Jacob. "Even with lower requirements, I am too old and too useless for Canada. If I cannot stay here, I must go to Goa. I went to the Indian authorities as soon as my citizenship was taken away. They said that they would help me go to Goa as a special case, although they will not say this in public. They will give me a travel document to go to Goa."

"That's good," said David. Maybe there was some good in the Indian authorities after all and Josephine was wrong.

"I was a good friend of your late father," said Jacob. "God rest his soul. I did many things for him, and he did many things for me. Now I would like you to do one thing for me."

"Of course, I'll do what I can," said David. "If you need an air ticket ..."

"No, I have enough money for an air ticket," and Jacob. "I was saving for a two-way ticket so that I could go to Goa on a visit, but I never made it. I have also saved three thousand shillings. This money is to be used to pay for my funeral expenses. But now I have to leave for Goa, I will need this money to pay for the funeral there. I don't have any relatives. I have never sent money out of the country. Can you help me send this money out to Goa for me?"

David was taken aback. He wanted to help but he, too, had never sent money out of the country illegally.

"I'm not asking you to send the money out through the back door," said Jacob. "I have heard that the government might let civil servants who were not citizens retire and take some of their benefits with them. If you know of anybody from your Department or any other Department who does not have as much money as he is entitled to take out, please tell him to take this money for me. I will come for it in Goa."

Jacob was right. The government had just taken such a decision. David racked his brain to find someone honest and thought of Ramos Pacheco. He was not too sure that anyone else would give Jacob the money once he was out.

Jacob told David that he had just sold his Bedford van to one of the market Damibians for fifty shillings. "I wanted to give it to him but he insisted on paying," said Jacob with a smile. "He even wanted to pay Shs.100, but I could not accept more than the commercial value of the van."

Jacob left two days later, carrying an old battered case which did not uppear to contain much. He was wearing the same old shabby brown outfit and his American-detective hat. He walked up the stairs of the plane and at the top, in imitation of all the people he had seen leaving by air, gave one wave and was gone.

Three days later, the van broke down and could not be repaired. The people said that Jacob had died in the faraway country because he had lived in Lubele for as long as anyone knew. The remaining Goans heard the rumour and somebody said that actually Jacob must be alive and well, drinking *feinim* at the beach resort of Calangute, because be had never had a day's illness in his life. But the people said that just like the old Bedford, old Jacob had given up his spirit.

19

George Kapa heard the sound of a car coming up his driveway. He put off the light in the bedroom and looked out of the window. There was no harm in being cautious these days. It was a Ford Cortina. Looked like David D'Costa. He went and opened the front door. It was David. This was a little unusual because, although they were friends, David did not visit. George unlocked the door.

David entered, greeting George and Miriam, his wife. "What drink will you have?" asked George.

"Beer will be fine," said David, sitting down and staring at sticks hanging against the wall. Little beads, white, blue and black, had been threaded in an intricate pattern around the sticks. They were made by George Kapa's tribe. "Say, George, can you get me some of those beaded sticks? As a souvenir."

"Souvenir?" asked George. "You're not going away, are you?"

"I'm afraid I am," said David. "And that is what I have come to tell you. Josephine and I have just decided to leave Damibia."

"What!" said George, half-rising out of his seat. "You're not serious!"

"I am," said David, thanking Miriam for the beer and groundnuts.

"But *wapi*? I have always told my friends you are a greater nationalist than I!"

"I cannot take any more," said David. "I have already told you all my adventures over my citizenship, my passport, my attempts to get my wife her citizenship. And now, as you know, my citizenship has been taken away."

"But, man, didn't you always say that the situation of East Indians and Goans here is a political problem, caused not by African hatred but by the British colonialists, who need scapegoats? Didn't you say that decolonization is always painful, that one must expect all kinds of apparently absurd sufferings after Independence? *Rafiki*, isn't this the same thing? Be consistent! You have been exempted from leaving!"

"Yes, but my effort to get an identity card, even after my application for exemption was approved, was another story by Kafka. I had to spend two days at the Immigration Department.

The last-minute photographs cost us Shs.20 each at an African photographer's while Tony Fernandes used to charge Shs.10. I had to join five queues at the Immigration Department, one to be registered, another to pay my fee, a third to try and get the identity card, and two more to get identity cards for my wife and kids. Twice, because I was stateless, the people at the counter refused to serve me. I had to wait and plead and plead with other, more sympathetic, faces. Look at my identity card, which only East Indians – citizens or not – have to carry. I got it today."

David handed over a thick blue card, roughly bound with the same materials as had been used to bind the law books. The government printer must have used law-book leftovers. George looked at it carefully. It had a photo of David and various details. In a section marked "Nationality" it had written on it "Damibian" but this was cancelled and replaced by "none".

"Looks like it's bullet-proof," said George.

"Yes," said David wryly. "After the Deadline, four days from now, the soldiers will not have to stop us. They will just shoot at our hearts and those who survive will be the ones carrying these cards in their breast pockets."

George kept staring at the card, shaking his head and clicking his tongue in disapproval.

"I have always been opposed to institutionalized discrimination," said David, "which is why I oppose South African apartheid and the pass system. This is the same thing."

"No, it is not," said George, handing the card back. "Of course, it is terrible. But man, we are all suffering. You know that after the Deadline, if your political theory is right, there will be no East Indian scapegoats. The people do not in fact hate East Indians. You will be able to present a case and get back your citizenship. Why are you not willing to have your share of suffering? Why equate yourself with a non-citizen *dukawalla*? Only here while the going was good and when there is trouble leave?"

"Today Kisirwa announced that there were only four days left for East Indians to leave the country. Did you hear the latest announcement by the General? Made it while speaking to some athletes."

"No, I haven't tuned in to the news."

"Well, I listen to the news. Every East Indian and Goan listens every day!"

"Do you remember at university, East Indians couldn't understand why we used to listen to the news everyday, trying to find out what was happening in the Congo, in the British Parliament over the constitutional conferences, and elsewhere. It was 'only politics'."

"True," said David. "Politics is a dirty game you should ignore only when it doesn't affect you. When it does, you get politicized fast! Anyway, the General said that all East Indians who stay behind after the 21st will be sent to villages to integrate with Africans."

"So? You always said that East Indians are to blame for not integrating with the indigenous people!"

"Do you know where he wants to send us? To Warajojo! Warajojo, where there is still cattle raiding, where the people do not accept Damibians from other areas of the country, where they still carry spears everywhere, every day..."

"Hey, Dave, the General is pulling a fast one. Don't you remember he said that he would get rid of East Indians by using military tactics? Psychological tactics are military tactics. No doubt he learned them on training abroad. Remember those photos of the General visiting concentration camps for East Indians who do not leave? They were not camps but hospitals, new hospitals that hadn't been opened. I know. I visited with the Chief Water Engineer to check on them."

"But how do I know he does not mean it this time? If he is anxious that all East Indians should leave, what if he suddenly cancels the exemptions and tells us to quit in 24 hours? Can I play with the lives of my wife and daughter – children – on the chance that my idealism is correct and not their fears?"

"So that's it!" said George triumphantly, putting down his beer. "Your wife! You know, I'll never understand Goans! You are patriarchal, like all East Indians, but over critical issues you are ruled by your women! Miriam would never be able to get me to change my mind about anything, once I had made it up. I am the boss and there's no two ways about it."

"But I would be selfish to gamble..."

"Jesus!" said George, jumping to his feet and moving to face the mask hanging on the wall. "Why should women and children be exempted from the problems of mankind? If there's a political crisis, it affects everybody! For only men to take risks and women and children to be given an exemption from danger? Be realistic, man! In every war, women and children face the same problems as everyone else." George went to the window and looked out, listening abstractedly to the chirping of crickets.

"Not the same!" said David, indignantly.

"Ah ha!" said George, looking into David's eyes. "You are afraid that your wife will be raped. And raped by an African, which is far worse! After all, you are also a racialist!"

"Damn it, George, rape is rape whoever the rapist! Don't talk so casually. You can afford to talk lightly..."

"I'm sorry," said George, sitting down. "I did speak too casually. But are you facing any greater dangers than the indigenous people of Damibia? Haven't many Damibians, indigenous Africans, been killed? Didn't you tell me that assassins have been after the head of your department for several months? Why, I may one day disappear without even a death certificate so that Miriam won't get my inheritance. You have to earn your citizenship by suffering, as you so often said."

"What citizenship? It was taken away, and nobody raised a finger to stop it. There must be some point to the suffering. No good will come out of this irrational, greedy regime, propped up by non-Damibian mercenary soldiers quite happy to suck the blood of the Damibians. I do not see any possibility of my being able to change it."

"So you want to run away! Where will you sneak off to?"

"Canada has come in and is taking away East Indians. They have lowered their entrance requirements. In any case, I will have no problem being accepted. The Canadians have objected to the General's directive that half the cost of the airfares of people being taken to Canada be paid to the local airline, so they are now taking East Indians free to Canada. One must assemble at the Independence Hotel in Blanwa the night before and one is taken in a bus to the airport, escorted by Canadian officials and police. And the Canadians have offered to find jobs for any East Indian who leaves for Canada with the teams before the Deadline – which is four days from now."

"Can it be that the West is now so humane?" asked George, sceptically. "You used to say that the Western countries were exploiters. Are you now saying that you were wrong?"

"Maybe Canada is more humane than the rest of the West," said David. "It too is exploitative, but it has a more humane for-eign policy than most Western countries. On the other hand, this is a great labour-recruiting exercise for them. See how many qualified doctors, lawyers, teachers, computer experts, lecturers, not forgetting the unskilled but experienced mechan-ics, plumbers, etc. they are getting for the price of a plane fare. And I must not overlook civil servants. What a great gift from the underdeveloped to the developed! From the early sixties, the Canadians have been recruiting housemaids from the West Indies. So Canada is probably self-serving while making this look like an exercise in humanity. But it also serves my inter-ests so why..."

"So when it comes to a crisis," said George, "you could not live up to the grand ideals you used to speak of! You are willing to leave your friends and your country!"

"George, I supported Mbuyiseni and his socialistic mea-sures, though I thought he went too slow," said David. This had been an area of disagreement with George. George thought Mbuyiseni capable but felt strongly that he was go-ing too fast with his socialism. George had not been unhappy at the overthrow.

"Mbuyiseni was overthrown," continued David. "He lost. My side lost. Throughout history, losers must give up, must retreat to lick their wounds."

"Are you doing that?" asked George. "You are running away. I thought you were a fighter. You stood up to the chal-lenges from all the older Goans..."

"I clashed with and criticized many Goans, and I disagreed with many Indians, but they are still my people. Our quarrels were family quarrels. I don't think I could live in any coun-try where there weren't at least some Goans and some Indians. Out of about 50,000 Indians and Goans who were Damibian cit-izens, the Immigration Department has dispossessed 45,000, to say nothing about the 60,000 whose applications for citizenship were disowned..."

"You can't mean seriously that you will miss people like Gerson Mendonca!" said George.

"Isn't it ironical!" said David with a smile. "The General did Gerson a favour. Gerson had applied twice in the past to Canada and had been rejected on medical grounds and because he had no special skills or education. Thanks to the General, the Canada entrance requirements were lowered, and Gerson was accepted today! He is getting ready to leave tomorrow. And despite all his money, years of saving and a big dowry his wife brought with her – that is why he got married – he is getting a free plane-flight to Canada! Yes, I would miss even Gerson Mendonca."

"I don't understand you, David. Aren't I your friend? Don't you have many Damibian friends like me?"

"History has caught up with us again. We have to run, as we have been doing for hundreds of years since the Portuguese conquered us. My mother would have been thrown out too, if she weren't already out of the country. She was in Goa when the expulsion order came. Africans have strong family ties. You know I wouldn't be able to live here if she couldn't."

"You will be able to bring her back when things cool down, surely."

"I'm not a hero, George. There must be some point to suffering. I am willing to make sacrifices if the masses can benefit. As they would have done under Mbuyiseni's socialist measures, given time."

"There you go again!" interrupted George, irritated. "Why must you be so idealistic? So impractical and abstract? With you, it's all or nothing. It's always been so. Why can't you just live and let live?"

"Damn you, George!" said David, losing his temper with George for the first time. "It's because of people like you that the General got into power!"

"Me?" said George, incredulous. "What did I have to do with it?"

"You, yes, you! You, the spoiled elite, who want the good life! Who pay lip-service to the people but who are opposed to their interests when they clash with your desire for luxuries! You were against Mbuyiseni not because he wasn't socialist enough but because he was too socialist. You didn't mind him being called 'socialist' if this were only a catch-word, a fashion. But when he started to take action, to cut down salary increments, to increase income taxes on higher incomes, to increase the customs duty on big cars, to ban luxury items like those imported Van Heusen shirts you loved from university days, to take a controlling interest in the banks that always gave you loans and overdrafts to build houses and buy second cars, you were against it. You were for cocktail socialism, the kind that American, Gerry Kern, exports. For you, 'socialism' was to be a ladder for catching up with the West: for your own interests. You wanted all the toys of the West. Thanks to you, to a thousand George Kapas, corrupt people in the old regime went in for television stations, television sets that only the elite could afford, for irrelevant imported comedies, luxury villas, and so on. Until the masses got totally sickened and cynical about the old regime. You turned Independence from a golden orange to a rotten apple. The foreign interests knew, thanks to a thousand George Kapas, that they could use the General to overthrow Mbuyiseni and his system, his nascent system, and the people would not be able to raise a finger to stop it."

George was taken aback. David had never before seriously disagreed with him, never before attacked him. The words had come spilling out, like a sudden Damibian thunderstorm. Always, David had appeared to be cautious about George's feelings, as though if he criticized George it would give the impression that he was anti-Damibian, anti-African. But when George criticized David, David fell onto the defensive.

"Foreigners were behind the coup," George conceded mildly, regrouping his forces behind the words. "But how is the General protecting foreign interests with his brutal, crazy actions?"

"He just got out of control once he got swollen with power, once he saw how much control he had over the actions and lives of the people in the country," said David. "The foreign interests miscalculated: they thought they could control him because he was so greedy and stupid. They forgot that even a stooge must have minimal intelligence, to be able to understand the system and to make choices which are rational from his own point of view. But, in the first place, the coup could only take place because the foreign interests knew that the George Kapas would be dancing in the streets, or rather, driving along the streets with branches and flags on their Peugeots 504. You wanted to keep the good life. The General was weak for the first four months. Your support, or indifference, gave him time to become strong."

"*Wacha*, Daudi!" shouted George, his blood rising. "You are only rationalizing your Goan habit of thinking small. You only have a small Ford Cortina because your Goanness and the rule of the Catholic make you feel that it is a sin for you to have anything bigger! I am not to blame for the General's actions! I have no tribal or race feelings!"

"No, but you have class feelings. Why did you not get involved in a mass movement? You have the easygoing liberal tolerance that is purchased by privilege. If you had started a mass movement I would not be sitting here trying to say goodbye! I am leaving because of you ..."

"Goddamnit" said George, leaping up. "You are passing the buck, blaming me for your own cowardice. Aren't you as a Goan a member of the privileged class?"

"Yes, and that is why you like the Goans – because they are still, to your not-yet-decolonized mind, the privileged class!"

"What about yourself?" hooted George. "Did you get involved with the masses? You have servants, and I bet you do not pay them a fair wage, in spite of all your talk about the masses. You contributed to your own isolation from the people, in spite of your fine words! Don't play more sinned against than sinning. You are only crying foul because things did not go your way. You are as guilty as everyone else. I ought to throw you out for being a hypocrite!"

Miriam was watching in trepidation from the doorway of the kitchen, wondering whether to discreetly retreat or to intervene.

"Hells bells!" said David, agonized. "What could I do?" He thumped his fist into his palm. "I could not start a mass movement, as a Goan. All I could do was support one when it started. That is what I did with Mbuyiseni's socialism. It was not much, but it was all that was available. As for my servants, I give them a fair wage within the system. I cannot give them any better as long as the system is unchanged. The system does not change if I give them a higher wage. But you, you are a black man, you come from a peasant background, you could have used your education to change the system. Doesn't an engineer want by his very profession to change and build things for the people? Instead of which, you settled for your own egoistic, selfish, debauched way."

"This is what I get from someone I thought was different, nonracial!" said George, leaning back in his chair and passing his hand over his eyes. "It's always the same old shit against Damibians and Africans. Whether it's 'white colonial racism' or 'socialism and the masses', it is the same thing: we black men are told not to be achievers. It's all right for an East Indian to own a shop and exploit, but let a Damibian try to own one and then the 'progressive' people and 'friends of Damibia' cry, 'No! The state must take over in the name of socialism, to end exploitation!' It's all right for a qualified Indian water engineer to earn a high, expatriate salary, but George Kapa, because he is a black Damibian, because he is an African – no, it is George's fate to be as poor as every African on this continent. It doesn't matter that he had to struggle through decades of education, walking miles to school and back on an empty stomach every day, working with the land to earn enough to pay school fees, and what for? So that he can suffer for all time! That is the way God and Karl Marx planned it, don't you see! The White God and the White Socialist Father!"

"Thanks to your ideological fuzziness, people like Al Kamena can keep fooling around. And the Gerry Kerns can become millionaires. And the General can be put into the saddle, trample on the backs of the people, and bring the whole building tumbling down on everybody's heads."

"It's the same old rubbish!" said George bitterly. "All Europeans and East Indians want Black people to be the hewers of wood and the drawers of water for all time. Not the building contractors and water engineers. And I thought you were different! To be abused in my own house! This is the thanks I get for liking Goans."

"Ha, some liking!" said David scornfully. "You have not come to the Institute to say goodbye to even one Goan, not even to your 'good friends' Joe Pereira and Cajetan Oliveira, who regularly played tennis with you. You did not come to the Institute on Sunday, when a general farewell party was held!"

David had hit below the belt. George recoiled. That really hurt. He had been afraid, afraid of what could be done to him after December 21st, after the East Indians and Goans were gone, if some thug of the General said that he had been seen fraternizing with the expellees, feeling sorry for them. He shook his head like a punch-drunk boxer. "This is the thanks I get for saving the Goan Institute," he said.

"Yes, the Institute and you," said David, cooling down. "As you know, I have a responsibility for the Institute as a Trustee, although I am not the President. I want you to take over the major responsibility for the Institute when I leave because then I know it will be in good hands. Then I know the Institute will survive, that the spirits of the Goan pioneers will have a home, that the Goans – like my father – will have made a lasting contribution to this country, however small. You are popular with nearly all members, including Goans. I've told you that if you weren't out of the country attending a conference when the last Annual General Meeting took place you would have probably been elected President, the first indigenous Damibian President of the Lubele Institute, after being the first Vice-President."

"Okay," said George grimly, thinking back to the days of his vice-presidency and to the times he had to suffer quietly by David's side while he delivered a very Goan speech to a very Goan audience. He was still tempted to throw David out of the house. But David got up to leave.

20 "East Indians are reminded that only two days remain before the Deadline. They must remove themselves from Damibia by two days from now," said Thomas Kisirwa, ending the ten o'clock news.

The crowd around the television set sighed and turned away. The television set had been moved from the T.V. room to the Institute's bar so that members could watch the late news as they drank. David D'Costa ordered another round of drinks for everyone in the bar and in the Institute. Ronald was serving behind the counter. People placed their orders.

David D'Costa and family were leaving! The few remaining Goans and the Damibian members could not believe it. David's late father had been President of the Goan Institute several times and the Goans thought he followed in his father's footsteps. Even when they opposed him for being an upstart and not going by tradition, they thought he was carrying his father's spirit. The departure of David, of all people, seemed to be the utter end of an epoch for the Goans, the absolute end of the Goan presence in Lubele. The Goans had always thought that it would come to this – that David loved Damibians blindly, that he did not see their faults and would have a rude awakening one day. Still, they did not believe that he would leave. After all, he was a fairly high civil servant and was earning a good and safe living. All the remaining Lubele Goans were at the Institute that night to bid him farewell. It was now the custom to find out who was leaving and then come to the Institute at night to have a drink with him and bid him farewell.

George Kapa was putting away beers like there was going to be a shortage of drinks after the Deadline. When he had received his special round from David, he clapped his hands and asked for silence. "I have known David from the days when we were students together, from the days when we were young, idealistic, innocent students!" George had begun a speech, although he did not like making them. "Although I must add that David was more idealistic and innocent than myself!"

Everybody laughed, but stopped immediately.

"I am sorry about the whole situation. Of all people, it really upsets me to see David leaving. David and I have been brothers, we have even quarrelled like brothers." George put away what was left in his beer mug and Ronald rushed round to refill it. "This, this is a great patriot. This is a great loss to the country!" George swayed dangerously. "I am a water engineer, although you might think right now that I am a beer engineer! By my training, I must think of building for the people, for the future. I must be optimistic about the future. So I must wish David and his charming wife Josephine ..." he turned to bow to Josephine, nearly falling as he did so "... and his children a happy future in Canada. I say that I must do this. But if I am honest, I must say to David..." he turned to David and looked him in the eye "... Damibia is your home. No castle, however luxurious, can be the same thing as home. An intruder can make home uncomfortable for a while, but intruders are finally ejected. Scoop out what you can in Canada and bring it home! At least you will have an address for a while and people will be able to write to you."

David had to reply. He said that although he had made several speeches and could speak at the drop of a hat, as all people present knew, this was the most painful time of his life for making a speech like this. "I had never expected that I would have to make a farewell speech, a speech when I myself was leaving." He said that he had been President of the Institute twice and although he had been accused of being high-handed, he could say that he had never done anything in bad faith and without getting the support of the majority of the members.

"I believe," he said, "that someone who tries to rule without the wishes of the majority of the people may appear to be successful for a while, but in the long run, the wishes of the people matter. This is why, although this is a sad moment, we must remember that the world is not coming to an end, that the sun always emerges after an eclipse. On behalf of Josephine, and Sharon and Felix, I wish this country a long and prosperous future, and when I speak of the country, I speak of the people. I will never forget Damibia." David stopped and drank, his eyes glinting.

"One thing more!" shouted George, through the clapping and weeping of the people. "I have a small gift for David here. My wife will present it."

Miriam came forward and presented Josephine, David, Sharon and Felix each a beaded stick. Each stick had a motif in black, green and brown.

"The three colours are to remind you of your three parents," said George. "Miriam made them specially for you. The three parents are your father Goa, your stepfather India, and your mother Damibia."

David did not normally cry, but he shed tears now. Even Josephine dabbed at her cheeks as she and David were embraced by sobbing people.

People carried on drinking until well after the legal hour for closing the bar. David only left finally because Josephine reminded him that he had not quite finished packing and they were leaving for the Independence Hotel in Blanwa the next day, to leave for Canada the day after.

21 "These students!" raged the General, his face bloating with rage. "Nothing satisfies them!" When he came into power they said he was reac – reac – something not very good. Some of them wanted President Mbuyiseni still and they ran away into Leshona. But even the others said they were not happy when he praised Britain and South Africa.

"Why should I not praise these countries? Look how much they have developed. They have big planes, big cars, lots of hotels, weapons, tanks, transistor radios, television. What do we have? But no, the students did not like it. My Minister of Overseas Affairs started telling me that I should become 'progressive' or I would be hated by all of Africa. He told me that I should not support the people who had milked the cow of the economy. I had never seen them milking the cow, but that is what he told me, and he has studied in big, big places. He told me that I should not have changed some of the things that Mbuyiseni did, that I should not listen to Moore-Diamond and Michaels. He said that Mbuyiseni was clever: he did the things that Africa would like."

The General was watching the 6 p.m. television news, hoping that it would carry a message of support from the students of Damibia University. Instead, Kisirwa said, "To end the news, East Indians are reminded that they have only two days left for the Deadline."

"Bah!" The General leaped up and snapped the television off, breaking off the knob. No wonder. It was the work of that Zionist agent, Kerensky, who had given him the set. "Now I am very progressive where are the students? All of Africa is singing my praises for throwing out the East Indians who were milk like the cows – milking the cow of the economy." He sometimes had trouble with those words. "Even some Black Americans have sent me praise and thanks. But nothing from the students! They are useless! They must be supporting Captain Oma! They must be made to show support for my policies! Soolooomoooon! Solomon!"

"Yes, your Excellency, V.C.!"

It was announced on the radio and television news at 10 p.m. that the students were going to have a demonstration of support for the General on the main street of Blanwa the following day. The soldiers went to the university and rounded up the students. They were taken to the main university square, where a roll call was taken by a quivering Registrar. The students were piled into army buses and driven, in their undergraduate gowns, to the edge of the city. They had to walk into the city. The townspeople saw a whole line of students carrying banners like "Exploiters of the people, stop your dirty work". But no sign carried the word "Indian".

A whole street had been blocked off for the demonstration and microphones had been assembled. When the students reached the place, opposite Clothing Inc., one of the largest shops and supermarkets in the city, they spread around, talking among themselves. The road had been widened to take the tanks of the General on the first anniversary of the Liberation from Dictatorship. The job had been done very speedily, to a cost of Shs.3,000,000. The road now looked like the top of a massive fruit cake, with bumps and pot-holes.

There was a roar. Vroom vrrrooommm! There was the General whizzing up on his Jeep, the action that had so impressed the people when he had just taken over! It showed he was one of the people, unlike his predecessor who did not drive around on Jeeps.

The General drove up to the V.I.P. stand in the car park opposite Clothing Inc. He went up before the microphone and, cocked hat on head, hand on holster, thanked the students for coming to demonstrate support for his policies. He said that he wanted the economy of the country to be controlled by Africans, and he was going to give first preference to Damibians and only then would he give a chance to other Africans.

"These East Indians," he said, "have cowed the milk – milked the cow of the economy for too long. It is only a fearless man like me who could take action to get rid of them. This is my one job in life and I do not care if I die after this job. I always do what God tells me. Now, I will listen to you."

The student leader, Magambi-Mukono, went to the mike and read out from a sheet of paper. He said that the students had always advocated the ending of exploitation. They had always wanted the control of the economy of Damibia to be in the hands of the people. But they did not want to exchange Brown or White exploiters for Black ones. For this reason, they proposed that the control of the economy be passed on to the cooperatives and the state corporations. They also urged that a government office be set up to supervise the state corporations, and that this office be made accessible to the common people. This was not enough, but it would be a start.

"As for East Indians," Magambi-Mukono said, "those who are not citizens of Damibia would have to leave one day, when they ceased to serve the interests of the country. What is important is to see that they leave with kind and fair treatment."

"As for the citizens, Your Excellency," – he stressed "Your" – "we, the students, urge you not to expel them. Let those who have already left return. We are not racists. We are opposed to exploitation. We do not think oppression and exploitation wear only one colour. We oppose racial discrimination in all forms, whether practised by White people against Black people, Brown people against Black, or by Black people against Brown."

What! thought the General, leaping up, hand on holster. Would they dare oppose him? Would they still support Captain Oma? He would get the student who dared call himself a leader at the party at the International Hotel. He would not do anything now, with the television cameras on him. But he would have to show firmness.

He went up to the student and grabbed the mike from him. "Thank you for your support," the General said. "The points you have raised, in expressing your support, will be given due consideration. But you are children and do not know the ways of the world. God Himself told me to get rid of all dangerous East Indians." How could he convince these stupid children? "Did you know that the Indians were planning to take over full control of the country, like the Europeans in Rhodesia?"

Warming to his subject, he went on: "Four years ago, I saw a group of Indians marching on Main Street on our Independence Day. I stopped and asked them what they were doing. They said, 'We are getting ready to take over.' I immediately ran to see President Mbuyiseni to tell him about this danger and that we must do something. He just laughed. He said, 'If I take action against the Indians, it will be the start of World War Three.' So, to save the country, I had to take over."

The General had forgotten that one of the Twenty-Four Reasons given for his takeover was that President Mbuyiseni had started phasing out East Indians who were not Damibian citizens and thus disrupting the economy. He had also forgotten that the last time he had spoken he had said that he had pleaded that he did not want to take over the government but the soldiers had held him prisoner for ten hours and only then had he agreed to save the country.

"The East Indians will be gone by tomorrow," said the General. "You are too young. Study, look after yourself, and leave the running of the country to your elders, who know these things." His hand strayed to his holster again. "See the doctors to make sure that you do not pollute the people of this country."

The General saw grins breaking out on the faces of the students. "All the fault of that student leader!" fumed the General. He would get him. "And now there is a party for you all at the Damibia International Hotel!"

The General jumped into his Jeep and roared off, waving his blue cap, tyres squealing as he turned round the corner at fifty miles per hour. The students followed on foot, discussing the General's speech.

"We are in the grip of an incomprehensible demon," said one student.

"He has fastened himself on us like a dreadful nightmare, like a vampire," said another. All offer him what I call the L.C.C., which means 'Lowest Common Civility', below which he would be merely an animal and not human."

"I come from a poor family," said a short, rough student dressed in a green shirt and khaki trousers. "My parents are peasants. Two shillings means four hours of hoeing. They can afford to buy only what is necessary. They pay their taxes at the beginning of the year and are terribly pained to see public money squandered on Mercedes-Benzes, Jeeps, arms to only terrorize and kill. Under the General, school fees have gone up, taxes have gone up, the export profits have gone down, new hospitals have not been opened and old hospitals are short of drugs. He is building a big new hotel in our area, constructed by Yugoslavs or some other Eastern Europeans. And now he is committing haemorrhage by kicking out all the East Indians."

"Did you hear him say he would give a chance to non-Damibian Africans to have the shops?" said a slim, long-faced girl. "It will be like his army and Tonton Macoutes. Blacks exploiting blacks with impunity. The Indian *dukawallas* did not dare exploit too much."

"The British and the West were keeping the General as a trump card," said a short, black student with frizzy hair sticking out like ferns. "But he got out of hand and bit the hand that fed him."

"The trouble with the General's regime is the General himself, not the East Indians as such. His ignorance in matters of state is abysmal. He goes to the O.A.U. meeting and tells heads of state that he could conquer South Africa with 200 soldiers in two hours. We have become a laughing stock."

A thin, vicious-looking student with a very flat nose and long arms said, "To sum up, how can we be expected to support His Illustrious, the Illiterate, Ill-advised, Ill-natured, Ill-educated, Ill-bred, Ill-favoured, Ill-judged General, who has Il-legally Ill-gotten the title of His Excellency, the Military Head of State and the Supreme Commander of Damibia?"

22 The General was so angry that he nearly failed to make the turn round the roundabout. What was all that talk about the "common people"! Did they think he had become President for nothing? That he was going to give up everything and give it all to the people? Let them become Presidents if they wanted things! He was only going to give things to those who helped him. The squad would get that student leader! Just because he had been to university! If only that principal had given the General the Doctorate of Philosophy in Economic War, the students would respect him more. Well, the stubborn principal had paid the price. No, he would personally see that fellow was made to feel pain for what he had done.

The party began. There were beers, fried chicken, and pieces of steak for everyone. Outside the gate below the balcony, there were many Damibians in worn and torn clothes, looking on at the feasting and hoping that some of the feasters would pass some of the food and drinks on to them. Members of the General's assasination squad went around the gathering, trying to find Magambi-Mukono. They could not find him. They would get him.

They went to the university and strode into Magambi-Mukono's room. He was not there. They would watch and wait. That evening, a special edition of the university newspaper carried a news item about the General's speech and a copy of Magambi-Mukono's speech. The squad went to round up the members of the editorial board. They would merely toss them in the boots of their cars in the usual manner and drive them to where they could be dealt with. The editorial board could not be found.

The word went round the university that the student leader and the whole editorial board had gone underground.

In the morning there was another assassination attempt on the General: his helicopter was blown up in mid-air and the pilot and passengers were killed. The General was not in the helicopter. Captain Oma had come to get him at night after the student leader's speech. The General had leapt out of bed, gun blazing. Then he had jumped into his new Mercedes-Benz and driven off at top speed, followed at a discreet distance by his bodyguards. After driving fifty miles into the countryside, the General had turned back and returned. He had been too tired to wake up in the morning.

23 David did not resign in the normal manner from his Ministry because he was exempted and might be stopped. There were stories of teachers being taken off the plane as the Minister of Education knew how valuable they were. He wondered if Jules Tavares had been one of them. His advice to Jules may have been right after all, though Jules probably preferred to go after all the threats of genocide, barely disguised. David and Josephine had decided that he would take three days sick leave from his Ministry and leave quietly, sending his explanatory letter of resignation from abroad to salve his conscience.

Evaristo would take his dog, Snoopy, to the local Veterinary Department to be "put to sleep"; they were too attached to Snoopy to pass him on to another owner, who might mistreat him, or to just leave him locked up in the garden, as some East Indians had done. Evaristo was staying on to finish up matters. He would pass some of David's books to the local public library. Then he would pass the keys on to Ronald D'Mello, who would hand them in to the Ministry of Housing.

The morning of the departure, David explained the position to his cook and housegirl. They had known it from all the activity, all the packing and selling of old clothes, crockery, gramophone records, etc. He thanked them for their several years of devoted service and gave them each four months' salary as well as a chance to take everything still left in the house such as bedsheets, pictures, clothes, pots and pans. Snoopy, chained to the doorpost, looked subdued and miserable.

There was a crowd of Damibians around the house. David took a long look at the house. Josephine dabbed her eyes. She looked even sadder than David. David looked at the Christmas tree they had planted in their garden. They had saved it from last Christmas for this year. Well, this time Christmas would probably be a white, cold one in Canada, if it was not miles in the sky. There would be no Christmas *baksisi* for the cook and housegirl. David took out his wallet and gave the cook and housegirl an extra twenty shillings each.

"Bye-bye, Snoopy!" the children said, hugging the dog. He looked more miserable. David, Josephine and the two children got into the car hired by Evaristo. The gathering of Damibian men, women and children looked on silently as David D'Costa and family left Lubele.

24 George Kapa drove to the airport to see David D'Costa off. There had been stories two weeks ago that the buses of emigrants were stopped at the various roadblocks and robbed. George could not stand to see these buses; they reminded him of the Jews in Europe being carted off to Hitler's concentration camps to their deaths. But the comparison was not apt: the East Indians were actually being saved from death. At least, those of them who were not so poor that they had to travel by train to the coast of Mozania, from when they would go by ship to India. According to press reports from Mozania, when the trains stopped at some stations the soldiers went in and raped the women and girls, beat up the men, and stole the few possessions they were allowed to take.

George could not understand why the foreign papers kept saying that East Indians were hated fanatically by the Damibians and that the General had gained in popularity with his shrewd decision to expel them. The foreign press had printed photos of Damibians dancing with joy when the General announced his expulsion. Well, one could always get photos of Africans dancing and say that they were dancing for this or that reason. This was an old game of the colonialist press. In fact, whenever George saw these buses passing he was so ashamed that he tried to block them from his mind. And he noticed that the Damibians by the roadside stopped and watched silently.

George had not been to this airport earlier. A not-yet-opened aircraft engine workshop about a mile from the airport building was being used for the "expellees", a new word that appeared on the news these days. George drove along Chapel Road, round the curve, down the curve, and then down the slope leading to the hangar. A new car park had been hastily cut out of the waste ground near the lake shore. He parked and walked slowly over to the wire-fencing. He reached the gate.

"*Simama! Wapi wewe na kwenda!*"

Two soldiers in battle fatigues guarding the gate, rifles raised.

"*Ko ona rafiki.*" George knew it was not safe to reply in English when the army spoke in Swahili. Swahili had never really become one of the languages of Damibia, but as there was such a multiplicity of languages a kind of pidgin Swahili had become the *lingua franca*, mainly among the uneducated. Most of the soldiers were highly conscious of being uneducated. So they took every opportunity to humiliate those who could not speak Swahili. Moreover, today was the last day of the expulsion and the soldiers could be jumpy.

"You have a *Muindi* friend?" asked one soldier in some astonishment.

"Well, actually a *Mugoa* friend." George knew that although Goans were also lumped under the term East Indians, generally they were not disliked at all. This would be a safe reply. It was. "*Kuja*," said the soldier, opening the gate. "Do you have any identification?" George produced his driving licence, which had his name and photograph. He was let through.

George looked around, searching for David. There were two big sheds, one of them used to be a workshop and the other a hangar. The hangar was being used to deal with people while the workshop was piled high with suitcases, trunks, boxes, like a matchbox skyscraper. "Good Lord," thought George, "will they ever be able to clear those things? I doubt anyone will get anything. The army will steal it all." George had heard the previous day that some soldiers had gone to the airport when there was no flight and taken many of the boxes and trunks. Then they passed the word round that there were free things for everybody at the airport. Some of the people wanted none of it: they did not think of having things that had the taint of blood on them. But others were tempted at the thought of sewing machines, pressure cookers, etc. which they knew would not be available shortly.

People had gone on a shopping spree before the East Indians left. Meanwhile, the soldiers told the police, who were still law-abiding, that people were looting the property of the East Indians at the airport, and this would be bad for the image of the country. The police went along just as people had started to take things and arrested them: the ex-houseboys, garage attendants and ex-*ayahs*. The police took them to the jail and locked them up. Later, army personnel came over, forcibly took the keys from the police chief, took the prisoners out, and stabbed and shot them to death, not caring one bit for the screams of the wounded and dying though the police station and jail were just off the main road.

George peered around cautiously from behind his dark glasses. It wouldn't do for the army and security personnel to see him looking around. He gazed into the other building. Was it crowded! East Indians of all shapes and sizes and ages. There was an old woman, so old that George wondered whether she would be able to make it to the plane. She was limping around, bow-legged, helped by a young girl. There was a young Sikh in a smart bell-bottomed suit and wearing a turban. His beard was small and very neat; it looked like he had used an invisible trapeze net to hold it in place.

Strange, when George was young, he used to be afraid of these Sikhs, who looked very fierce and warlike and were all over the place. Unlike the other East Indians, the Sikhs came into contact with Damibians all the time because they were carpenters, lorry-drivers, contractors, plumbers, and even policemen. George had been to Malaysia last year and had seen that there were Sikhs in the police force there as well. The British seemed to like using Sikhs as policemen in the old days. Maybe it was easier to frighten the people with such a foreign and foreign-looking people. The Malaysians were even more terrified of the Sikhs than he had been. What would they think if they saw the Sikhs leaving Damibia so tamely? That the General was a real monster, to be able to subdue even these fierce people!

George was sure that this young Sikh was Gurmeet Singh, one of the national hockey players who had recently represented the country at the Commonwealth Games. The General had made an offer of citizenship to all the East Indians representing the country and he had paraded with them on their return, saying, "If all East Indians had been like these people, there would have been no problem." The General was a sports fan. Obviously, this particular hockey player had not accepted the offer.

George could see a makeshift table at the far end, where a customs check was taking place. There had been stories that the women had been completely stripped and searched because some of them had hidden gold round their bodies or even in their menstrual pads and up their vaginas. He could not see this happening here; maybe it had been only rumour.

"Sq–eea–allk! Bo-ooo-wwwww!" A groaning from the far end of the table. George's heart leaped up. What was going on? Oh, it was only one of the customs officers taking out a saxophone and blowing it, perhaps looking for hidden gold. He saw the officer handing it to the owner, a short, mustachioed man, and gesturing to him to play. It was Ramos Pacheco, who played for one of the well-known Goan bands, Nobby and his Nobs, after civil service hours. There must have been a farewell ceremony for Ramos at the Institute last night. Ramos had been a good and conscientious assistant treasurer.

Ramos took the saxophone and wailed out a whole verse of "St. Louis Blues". God, the man could play with feeling! George had never heard him play like this with Nobby and his Nobs. That blues had been George's favourite music ever since Louis Armstrong had visited the country in the early sixties. From Satchmo, George had learned that the blues carried the suffering of a people helpless against their problems and oppressed by the whole power structure but also the determination of the people to carry on living. Ramos must be hating to see the evening sun go down because not his baby but he would be leaving this town.

George was amused to see so many cloth and canvas bags tied with twine and string and so many blankets rolled into bundles. East Indians thought they were so different from the Damibians but actually they were the same. George was always embarrassed when he wanted his mother to come with him to Lubele and she came with all these bundles. She even did this when she travelled by taxi and George had to go to the taxi and carry out all the stuff. George himself, as a seasoned, modern traveller, always travelled light and smartly with two small suitcases and an attache case bought in New York. But perhaps these East Indians were taking a piece of the country, the touch and smell of it, which you couldn't do with modern valise cases and Samsonites.

David hadn't appeared. Oh, there in the distance, on top of the hill and near the fence of the former Minister of Citizenship and Internal Affairs, was a whole procession of vehicles and a bus. That must be him, escorted like a king. And he was a socialist, smiled George.

Suddenly, George heard shouts and thumps. He lowered his gaze to the gate. A black Damibian in black rags was just buckling at his knees. A soldier was near him, rifle butt raised. A smartly-dressed civilian African next to him raised his arm and gave the black Damibian a karate-chop on the back of his neck. The man collapsed like a sack of potatoes. Before he hit the ground, the soldier had struck his back with his rifle butt. As soon as the man was down, the soldier and the civilian kicked him over and over again with hob-nailed boots. "God!" thought George. "They are killing him in front of everybody!"

"He was trying to steal one of the bundles," said an African at George's elbow. George did not say anything. Like the other two, this man did not look like a Damibian. He could be an agent provocateur. George himself began to feel pains shooting up his back.

The man was then dragged to his feet, grabbed by the two men around the shoulders, and rushed to the gate, which had been opened for the new bus. He was thrown through the gate and sailed into the air, just missing the bus. "Just like a plane taking off," thought George. But amazingly, he saw the man pick himself off the ground, wipe the blood off his forehead and nose, and then stumble off. "The people have a lot of endurance!" thought George, admiringly, "The General will find that it is not easy to kill everyone in this country." Maybe David was right – he should have identified more with the people than with the toys of the West.

The bus was through the gate and the passengers were getting off. Some of them looked like Damibians, Africans, with dark skin and kinky hair. Maybe they were half-castes. The General had extended his decision three days ago to cover those people in Damibia who were "of East Indian origin, extraction or ancestry". This meant, in effect, that anyone who had as much as one East Indian grandparent had to leave. Many such people had considered themselves indigenous Damibians, Africans, and had never gone to the Citizenship Department to apply for citizenship. They had to leave now. So much for the General's occasional accusations that the East Indians had not integrated and intermarried. Those who had still had to leave and so had their offspring. There was a black woman! Could she also have an East Indian ancestor?

A few years ago, a group of very Indian-looking Indians had come from India to Damibia, saying that they were trying to trace their African ancestors who had gone to India from Eastern Africa in the sixteenth century and intermarried there. It seemed that there were no racial problems in those days. No, George could not believe that the black woman had any East Indian blood – or, more correctly, genes. She was wearing a sari, but wearing it badly, as though it were a *busuti*. Maybe she is trying to convince people that she has Indian blood because she does not have any; maybe she is so scared of what the army will do after tomorrow that she is running away while she can.

Ah, there were David, Josephine and their children getting off the bus. The daughter was carrying a doll and the son a locally woven cot for the doll. George checked his impulse to rush to the bus and waited for them to get off and join the end of the queue. He then went up.

"*Jambo*, Daudi!" he said.

"Who...!" exclaimed a startled David. "Why, George!" He looked like he couldn't believe his eyes. He made as though to embrace George, but he was too weighed down with a case, a camera and a transistor radio. "Good to see you, George," said David. "How is Miriam?"

"Fine!" said George. "She couldn't come."

"I know," said David. "You have come. I appreciate it, man!"

"Where's Evaristo?" asked George.

"I told him not to come," said David. "He is staying on to sort out our affairs. He'll join us after that. He'll go to Goa first to collect my mother and bring her along."

What could one talk about at a time like this except the most literal facts and the most banal clichés, hoping that the feeling could be sneaked in under the words? "I wanted to bring you a final thing for good luck," said George. "You know, among our people, when someone is setting off on a long trip, to unknown territory, we believe in giving him something of the old soil so that he will still have roots. But I could not."

"Yes, I know," said David. It would not do for anyone, least of all a Damibian, to be accused of handing something to one of the expellees. David looked nervous and kept looking over George's shoulders, as though he expected someone to come along and stop him from leaving.

The queue was inching forward. George moved to one side.

George was growing impatient. David was probably used to this business by now. He had to join queues nearly everyday for the past few days. He had to queue, first over checking his citizenship, then to get his exemption, then for his identity card, then for cards for his wife and children, then to be interviewed by the Canadians, then to get his emigration papers, then to get exchange control approval to take a travel allowance (which had been reduced to Shs.1,000 per family, one month's rent in Canada), then to be innoculated against yellow fever and smallpox, then to have his belongings accepted for airfreighting. And he was one of the lucky ones. What about Jackson Gomes? Jackson had to queue outside the British High Commission to see if he could get back British citizenship, since the Damibian authorities had taken his citizenship away on the grounds that he had not correctly renounced his British citizenship. After queuing for over a day, the British told him that he had in fact correctly renounced his British citizenship; the Damibians were not right to tell him that. As the British Home Office had stamped the certificate four months after his Damibian citizenship came through, the citizenship was invalid. He would have to take the matter up with the Damibian authorities, the British said.

"Might as well tell someone to talk to a hungry lion," Jackson had told George the night of David's farewell. "People have been beaten up just for looking suspicious near the Immigration Department." Jackson had to queue: the British would not accept him, the Canadians didn't want him, the Australians only wanted highly qualified doctors, the Indians said he was not Indian. The U.S. government took a decision to accept a thousand stateless East Indians with no qualifications. Jackson joined this queue, expecting to be asked "What did Lincoln say at Gettysburg?" and "When was George Washington born?" Instead, he was asked to prove that he was stateless. This he could not do. When it was too late for acceptance, he had proof that he was stateless: the letter from the Immigration Department asking him to remove himself from the country by December 21st. Jackson had left the day before for a U.N. camp in Austria, embittered with Damibia and Africa.

George had forgotten how to queue and was getting tired. He kept shifting from one foot to another. The only other time he had seen so many Indians was when he passed through Bombay on his way back from Malaysia. He hadn't known until then that there could be so many poor Indians in India. He thought that was why so many Indians had left their country and come to Eastern Africa. On the other hand, as an official visitor, he was taken to visit some of the factories and to have dinner with some of the owners. There he had seen wealth and luxury such as was well beyond the reach of even the wealthiest of Damibian East Indians. It all reminded him of the pyramids he saw at Giza, Egypt. The broader the base of the pyramid, the higher the topmost point was from the ground.

Wealth had certainly not saved the richest East Indian family, the Mankoos, a family of industrialists. The head of the family had been locked away in the Tokyo while the checking of citizenship was taking place. He was freed three days ago and told he was not a citizen because he did not have his papers checked. The whole Mankoo family was told to leave before the 21st. The General grabbed the big industries belonging to the Mankoo family or, rather, to foreign capital and run by the Mankoos.

Not that George had much sympathy for the Mankoos. It was true that they must have worked hard; the first Mankoo had walked in from the coast and walked around for hundreds of miles selling small things to the people. It was also true that all East Indian family businesses were run on small profit margins as they had low overheads and as the whole family worked. But they must have also bribed their way to success.

There were rumours about the "gifts" they had given politicians in the previous regime and, after the coup, it was rumoured that they paid the wages of the army for two months. And the General no doubt decided to grab the whole cake instead of taking slices.

No, what pained George was that the Damibian regime had no respect for international law. Once people were citizens, or had even indicated their wish to be so, Damibia had to keep its word. How could a man travel on a Damibian passport only to be told eight years later that he was not a citizen? And for no specific crime except that he had the wrong ancestors? There should have been specific accusations and trials. There even were many indigenous Damibians who were not worthy of being citizens. The General himself: he was rumoured to be sending cash in American dollars to a Swiss bank. Too many African, Asian and Latin American leaders did this – and then they died, leaving their ill-gotten gains to be enjoyed by the gnomes of Zurich and Europe. It was also said that the General was born across the border.

George pulled himself out of his thoughts. They were getting too dangerous. What if the soldiers near the gate could read them? His life would not be worth one shilling. He would be fed to the fishes in the lake across the car park.

David had at last been cleared by customs. But he was separated from George and they were not even within shouting distance. David waved. George nodded his head. David began to articulate something. George took it to mean that he had better go. George was not used to going to see someone off at the Damibian airport and then leaving before the plane took off. His feet were turning to lead.

David broke close to the rope fencing dividing him from George and croaked, "The General has destroyed us."

George looked around. Was that soldier eyeing him suspiciously? Maybe they would accuse him of stealing some property belonging to an East Indian. It was getting dark. George decided that he had better leave. He raised his arm to David and waved it back and forth, like a wiper brushing away the muck from a dirty windscreen. This was not the way to say goodbye, but he had made the gesture. They would meet again, if George lived. He waved his hand again and articulated the words, "See you!"

And then George turned and walked to the gate. The soldiers looked at him and asked him to identify himself. He produced his driving licence again. They looked at it and reluctantly opened the gate. "After tomorrow, eh, we will see whether the General is right or wrong. *Kwaheri!*"

George was startled. Was the man trying to trap him into making a statement against the General? He couldn't take a chance so he only replied "*Kwaheri*", walking to the park, half-wondering whether he would find his car. Once, his car had been stolen in broad daylight when he had gone to the Blanwa Post Office. The Damibian car thieves were real experts. They could make duplicate keys, steal wheels, strip down cars, and so on. When he had bought a new car with the insurance, he had fitted it with five anti-theft devices: a concealed key which cut off the ignition, a switch which caused the horn to sound off if the car were touched, a steering lock, a gadget which locked the steering wheel to the clutch, and round wheelnuts which could only be removed with a special spanner. Still, he had no doubt that his car could be stolen if the thieves wanted. And lately, they were doing it at gunpoint.

His car was gone! No, there it was, obscured by someone who had parked badly. These days, the car thefts had slowed down, probably in anticipation of the cheap and even free cars that would be available soon after the expulsion. But George knew that this was only a lull. In fact, once it was clear that the Indians were going, people had gone on a spending spree. Blanwa had become a beehive city for the past two weeks, like Cairo. The people somehow knew that there would be commodity problems after the expulsion and were stocking up. As for cars, there would not be enough Indian cars for everyone in Damibia who wanted one. When the lack of foreign exchange combined with the lack of experience and lack of sources of foreign credit for the new importers there would be an acute shortage of cheap cars – and then would there be car thefts!

As he started his car, George wondered whether it would not be safer to buy a bicycle. It had been fun in his younger days, and during his visit to America he found that it was no shame or loss of class to ride a bicycle. The people did it to keep in shape and he might have to do it as well, to keep in unshot shape. His Peugeot 504 would be in great demand. Wouldn't David find it ironical if he saw George on a bicycle! He would feel that George was being converted to his brand of ascetic socialism.

The evening mist had risen. He saw points of light across the lake, from the islands. Flashes of lightning, going to the bottom of the lake. One of those islands was the famous Rake Island, where that British diplomat had hidden while the country thought he had been kidnapped. How old that affair seems, he thought. That was one of his disagreements with the old regime: it made a fuss about small matters. A storm in a tea cup, while now there was a hurricane in a lake of blood.

He rounded the climb and the makeshift airport faded into the gloom behind him. Passing the brick-red Catholic church, he made a sign of the cross, wishing David a safe flight. Statistically, with so many East Indians leaving by air, there was a chance of at least one plane crashing. He had always wondered when taking off whether the plane would fail to make it and he would end up in a watery grave, fitting for a water engineer. These days, he seemed to think a lot about death. He had begun to feel that just to have a marked grave on land and relatives who could visit it was a luxury, like owning a car ten years ago.

George arrived home. He heard the screaming of a jet engine and a rumbling. A plane was taking off. Was that David's flight? He wished him well. But what the hell, he thought as he entered. The way things were going, it was no use being sentimental about David's going; he would probably have to quit himself. He did not see how the killings would stop. When things went wrong the General always wanted to blame someone and, by the laws of diminishing returns, George's turn would come sometime, although he was not involved in any kind of politicking. Better prepare himself for the time he had to leave in a hurry. That is, if any country would accept him. With all this foreign publicity about Damibians fanatically hating East Indians, he would be blamed for the expulsion and be told he had to live with the consequences of his inhumane action, just as after the General's public statement that he admired Hitler, the Damibian Embassy in New York had received eighty bomb threats from very active New Yorkers.

George switched on the television. Tom Kisirwa came on. "East Indians are reminded that today is the last day for their departure. They have four hours left. All who have not left will face the consequences."

George felt betrayed. He wanted to leave Damibia and shake its dust off his shoes forever. He had better start preparing himself psychologically for having to leave home.

"The General has let God down very badly," he said.

25 "God speaks to me," said the General, tapping his temple with his right forefinger. "God told me to get rid of the East Indians, and now they have gone."

Ronald D'Mello looked warily at the General to see if he was looking at him. It was the morning after the Deadline. Ronald had been sent by his Ministry, the Ministry of Public Information, to attend the opening by the General of the Damibian Development Bank. A government spokesman had said that this was Phase III of the General's Economic War. Ronald remembered that Mbuyiseni had spoken of setting up this Development Bank. "The General can get away with murder," Ronald thought, and kept a stiff upper lip because he knew the General *could* get away with murder. No, the General did not seem to be looking at Ronald. Either he was clever and had never hated East Indians or he saw what he wanted to see: he said there were no East Indians left and he therefore saw no East Indians. Or, maybe, he saw Ronald and thought he was an Arab.

"God speaks to me," repeated the General, tapping his temple once again. "When Ebrahim el Akbar came to see me from Al Azhar University – do you know Al Azhar University? – he told me that once every hundred years a great man comes on this earth to lead his people."

The General paused for effect.

Ronald wanted to laugh but knew he would be a dead man if he did. The crocodiles would chew on his bones. The other people present nodded their heads vigorously in assent.

"Development does not mean opening and occupying new buildings," said the General slowly, moving back to the text of his speech. It did not strike him that he was in fact opening a new building which was going to be occupied by a new bank. They were in a large boardroom on the sixth floor of this new building. The General went on stumbling through the words of his very leftist and nationalist speech, which was simultaneously issued to the press and television. The African press in other parts of the continent and the Afro-American press were impressed with the speech. But the General was not too impressed with it for he kept putting it down from time to time to speak his own thoughts. Every time he did so Ronald noticed that Abdul Aziz and James Wabinda winced. He also noticed the head of the Department of Civil Bureaucracy, David Michaels, blushing.

"I love you all!" said the General, extending his arms in a benediction. "I want to work for all of you. I am not a socialist, I am not a capitalist. I only want to work for my country." He smiled, but his eyes glinted. "I want all of you to work for the country. I do not want any politics. I do not want any quarrels. I do not want any useless talk. I do not want criticism."

"My God!" thought Ronald, glancing out through the window and becoming very aware of how high above the city he was. He could see the city park just below. He had come with the Ministry of Public Information television and radio units to record the General's speech at the opening of the bank. "I swear the General has bloated to almost double his size. He must weigh four hundred pounds at least!" The General's bodyguards had told Ronald's informants that everytime he had hallucinations about Captain Oma, he swelled up; as though he lost control of all his cells. This happened the last time he went to the hospital for mental treatment. Ronald's Ministry had to tell the nation that he was suffering from a sore throat.

"I want development," said the General, wagging his forefinger warningly at the people. "I do not want people to waste their time with useless things. No politics! I only want the truth. As for those people who were not interested in development, who were not interested in the truth, who were only interested in politics, where are they?" Ronald thought he saw Aziz and Wabinda hold their breaths. The General's eyes had become red and he snorted for a moment. Then he shook his head and went back to his paper, repeating a sentence he had read earlier.

When the speech was over, the General called out to his Overseas Affairs Minister, "Gowada!"

"Yes, your Excellency!" Lazarus Gowada had stood up. Jesus, even that bastard looks puffy! Is he going crazy too?

"Go and tell the Ambassador from South Arabia that I will be late for the meeting we had arranged for this morning. I will come after the celebration for opening this bank."

"Yes, your Excellency! At once!" And Lazarus sleepwalked to the door and exited, leaving his briefcase behind. It was discreetly picked up by an official from the Ministry of Overseas Affairs.

"Has the Ambassador already arrived?" thought Ronald, panic rising in him. "The Minister had said he was arriving day after tomorrow and arranged for photos and press coverage accordingly." It would be awkward if he had to run away only because the Minister of Public Information had made a mistake. Ronald had made a firm decision for the first time in his life. He had decided to stay on in Damibia, beyond the Deadline, come what may. His Damibian citizenship had been taken away because he could produce only a certified copy of his Certificate of Renunciation of British nationality and not the original. But this was his country. He did not have a wife and kids like David, neither was he a scaredy-cat like Joe. Both these great nationalists had sneaked out to Canada although they had been exempted. But Ronald had decided not to run away. He had been exempted and this was his home. There could be no escape hatches from home. David and Joe had placed themselves on the same level as Gerson Mendonca, who had never become a citizen so that he could leave when the going got rough. David had not even had the guts to resign properly and hand in his keys to the Ministry of Housing – he had sent the keys on to Ronald through his brother! That reminded him: he would have to hand in the keys to the Ministry of Housing when he got back to Lubele. David should not have left, thought Ronald sorrowfully. Today was the day after the Deadline and nobody had been hauled off to concentration camps or to villages.

People were walking out of the Conference Room in the wake of the General. Ronald walked out as well. He walked down the stairs, not wanting to be crammed into an elevator with dozens of people, like corned beef. Why, he might even find himself face to face with the General himself! No, he preferred to walk. He had better look for his colleague Moses

Maphele, to find out whether the Ambassador of South Arabia had in fact arrived. Moses would be at the party to celebrate the opening of the bank.

The party was held in the parking lot. It followed the familiar pattern of booze and eats, of people guzzling several bottles of beer and whisky. As usual, there were the poor outside, looking on at the feasting. The parking lot was bounded by tall buildings and the gate formed the fourth side of the box. Ronald felt that he was in a cage in a zoo, with all the people clinging to the bars and looking in. He found it impossible to eat anything or to do more than sip a bottle of beer. Periodically, the policemen would chase the people back from the gate to let in some dignitary, but the people would rush back.

There was a roar, like the whirling of a strong wind through Maba Forest. The General walked in regally. People rushed up to him, jumping up and down, some falling to their knees before him, waving their arms and saying, "Excellency!" "Our Leader!" "Our Saviour!" And the General walked forward imperiously, brushing through wave upon wave like an expert swimmer, like King Canute telling the waters to move back.

"Disgusting!" a voice whispered in Ronald's ear. Ronald almost jumped out of his skin. It was Moses Maphele. Moses had come to Damibia from Southern Rhodesia, or, as he preferred to call it, Zimbabwe, to escape White racist, fascist oppression. "Disgusting," said Moses again, softly. "When Mbuyiseni was in power, where were the critics? And the day he fell, it seemed like he was responsible for all that had gone wrong in this country, and that nobody had ever supported him! Just look at them!"

"Moses!" said Ronald. "Wasn't the Ambassador of Southern Arabia supposed to be coming day after tomorrow? Wasn't that what we were told? And we made arrangements..."

"Relax!" said Moses, patting Ronald's shoulder. "You are right. The Ambassador is coming on schedule."

"But then...."

"You should know the signs – the Big Man is beginning to lose his mind. What with all," he looked over his shoulder, "the blood he has spilt. He is losing his sense of time, of cause and effect."

"How do you know?"

"Have you ever read *Macbeth*? By Shakespeare?"

Ronald shook his head. "I always hated Shakespeare."

"So did I, until I acted in an African production of *Macbeth* in Zimbabwe. God, what an African play that play is! Compare Macbeth and the Big Man, the Big Man is following the path of Macbeth perfectly." He looked over his shoulder again, then went for a bottle of beer. Returning, he continued, "Down to getting rid of families of people he suspects and even consulting three witch doctors for reassurance."

"What?" said Ronald, turning to look at Moses. Moses had very bulbous eyes, which came across on T.V. like the eyes of a frog. No doubt this must have been because in Rhodesia he had to be able to see everything in order to survive.

"Shh!" said Moses, beginning to talk a little louder about how impressive the opening ceremony of the bank had been. Then he dropped his voice again. "I am using the term loosely. He told us about one of them today, the man who says he is from Al Azhar. It's all junk, of course. I am a Muslim myself and know that there is no such thing in Islam about the great man every hundred years. No, the bees are now swarming around the honey, but honey that other bees have gathered. There is that fellow from Cameroon, that defrocked Catholic priest who says he can raise people from the dead."

"Doctor James?" said Ronald, sipping his beer. Dr. James had just turned up. Kisirwa had read about him in the news. Dr. James had told the General that he was doing God's will and, since he did so, he had nothing to fear from his enemies. Kisirwa also said that the doctor had the power to resurrect people from the dead. The General had given Dr. James Damibian citizenship, one of the houses of the departed East Indians, and a bulletproof Mercedes-Benz.

"That's the man!" Moses said. "And then there is a fortune teller from my country, Dr. Gabriel Nangombe. He keeps travelling around the whole of Africa. Do you know he has been living in the Damibia International Hotel for three weeks now? And tipping the waitresses lavishly! And where does he get his wealth from?"

"You don't mean... "

"Of course," said Moses. "That's what I mean. The ceremony today was wonderful and it is a fantastic idea to have a Development Bank. As I have been telling you at some length, I hope that when my country, Zimbabwe, which is now called Southern Rhodesia, is independent, we too will have the foresight to have a Development Bank."

Ronald looked into Moses' eyes and saw the reflection of someone who had moved close towards them. Intelligence agent, probably. The only good thing was the General's intelligence agents did not live up to their name and one could spot them. All the same, he had better be careful, especially as he was a Goan civil servant. The agent would have to produce something to earn his keep. Ronald decided that he had better not look conspicuously different. He went over for another beer and began guzzling away until the man who had moved close edged away. Ronald then switched drinks, pretending that he was drinking whisky and ginger ale, but, in fact, only drinking plain ginger ale. Ronald had the feeling that if he ever got drunk around the General, he would yield to his deepest impulses and try to break the General's neck. Might as well snap off his own.

26 Two days after David D'Costa left, the Ministry of Housing came over to check whether his house was in good condition or not. The officials found that the servants' quarters were still occupied by two servants. They told the servants to leave the quarters within a day, with all their belongings, or else the police would be informed to come and throw them out.

27 Bwana D'Costa has gone. U-u-u-u-u-u- u – this *governmenti* has done very bad. I did *kazi* for his father a long time ago, a long, long time ago, when I was still a young boy. I had wanted to go to school but my father did not have money. I had to start working as a *shamba* boy and then as a houseboy and then as a cook, I worked for a Goan family, the Demerros, as a houseboy, and from their cook I learned to cook Goan food, to grind masala for curry every morning, to cook rice, and the other things the *Mugoa* like. The Demerros were not good people. They did not treat me as a man should be treated.

When I went to work for the Costas, they treated me well. I used to take sugar and a little meat sometimes. A man must live. Memsahib was *kali* when she found out, but Bwana Costa was a good man. He told her he would not be able to live on little money if he was a *pisi* and so they should not mind if I took sugar from here and there. So I stayed with them for many, many years. When they came to Lubele, I came with them, four hundred miles – he said – from my home. When he died, I stayed with his son. I am getting old now and I cannot work as I used to. What kind of work is it for a man to cook and look after someone else's house all his life? But the young *bwana* is good too. He treats me like his father. I was his father. I looked after him when he was a baby. He knows that I do not sweep all the house, but he tells the new *memsahib* not to scold me. Like the old *bwana*, he says that he would not like to work as a cook, and that the money they pay me is very little. It is very little, but it is more than other *governmenti* people pay, even some of my own people who yesterday lived in my village.

What kind of job is it for a man to work as a cook all his life? Who does not want a better life? To have a house, to have good clothes, to have a radio, to have a bicycle, to send the children to school and then to the big school so that they can become doctors or people of the *governmenti*? So that they can have big cars and live like the *Muzungu*? So that they can go to England in the big *ndege*? And then the whole family can go to the airport and see the *ndege* jump into the sky, near the lake? And wave and shake big cloths and weep?

I do not want a big car or house. I want only a bicycle and small house. I want enough to eat and drink. I want to be able to go home when I am tired. I have one son and he is going to primary school. I work hard for him, for my three children. Sometimes I drink a lot of *mwenge* and *waragi* and come home and make a little noise. What is it for a man to make noise? Why should people want to keep quiet always? Memsahib, she is *kali* and tells the *Bwana* she wants to sack me. He tells her that he would not like to work as a cook, and for so little money. He tells her to remember that if they lived in England, they will find that cooks cost too much money, so much that they will have to do the work themselves. I do not understand how this is; in England, they say, everyone is happy. Can you see Bwana sweeping the floor? When he goes many times to the *kilabu*? Memsahib thinks I do not see all these things.

To be a cook is no life for a man. But the *Generali* has done bad. He has told all the *Muindi* and the *Mugoa* to go away. He has told all the bad ones like Bwana Sequeira and the good ones like Bwana D'Costa to go. Why did he not tell only the bad ones go and the good ones stay? And what about the bad ones of our own kind? Some people of other villages treat *pisis* like me bad, bad, bad. They have *governmenti* houses which have houses for servants and *ayahs* and *pisis*. But they do not give them to us. They tell us to find our own houses, and they rent these houses to smaller people from the *governmenti*. They charge these people as much money for the small rooms as the *governmenti* charges them for the big houses! They think we do not know. But we see everything. And even some people from my village do this shameful thing.

Where will the *Muindi* and *Mugoa* go? Bwana Daudi was born here. I went to the *hospitali* when he was born. I carried him in my hands, I gave him bath. I used to give him my *ugali* to eat when he came to my house. I prayed for him when he was sick; when he came back from school, I used to ask him about it and about what he did there. He made *arusi* here, and he gave me a lot of money and food and things to drink – that day, I had to work hard, hard, hard. Does he have another home? Where has he gone? Who will look after him when he goes? Will Memsahib grind masala like I did to cook food for him that he will like?

And who will look after me? Where will I find a home? Where will I find a job? Who will give me a place to stay, *kazi* to do so that I can pay for my children to go to school? Who will teach in the schools now?

The *Generali* has done bad. He has killed *watu mingi, mingi, mingi.* Yesterday, his soldiers killed a priest. They stopped him on the road and shot him, cut his throat, and burnt his car. The radio of the *governmenti* said that he had been killed in a car accident. We know the truth. But who hears us? The soldiers kill, and kill, and kill. Before, we did not have much money, but we had life.

We could buy food, *matoke, samaki.* We could go home on taxis. We could send our children to school. We could go to the bars and meet our friends and stay with them for long, long time. We were not afraid, although there were some *kondos*. We were not afraid we would be found by other people in the lake. President Mbuyiseni did not kill us. But now, what has become of us? What will become of us? The *Generali* has done bad, bad. But Captain Oma is there. People have seen him. *Mungu* is there. One day, *Mungu* will hear our voice.

28 Two days after the Deadline, the Minister of Overseas Affairs and the Minister of Public Affairs went for a meeting out of the country and resigned from abroad, one pleading ill-health and the other accusing the General of being a monster who had wrecked the economy of the country and filled the lakes with too many bodies and too much blood. The General suspended his entire Cabinet. He announced that he was going to address the nation at midnight, December 24th.

29

These civilian Ministers are fools. When I gave them the jobs I made it clear that I am the government and the government is me. I made it clear that I am the chosen one, the prophet, the representative of God! Like my brother Moses from the land of milk and honey told me, our kind appear on earth once every one hundred years.

These people are fools. When I gave them the jobs, I gave them big and comfortable houses. I gave them big cars which were clearly written on and yet they could not see the writing. They were enjoying sitting in the cars but were too blind to read the writing on the wall of the cars. I even put radios in these cars so that they can talk to me, consult me wherever they may be. Now instead of doing that they start calling themselves my advisors! Who told them that?

These people are fools. Instead of carrying out God's orders communicated through me, the prophet, they waste a lot of tax-payers' money. They sit in the offices day after day, month after month, and write me a book which they call a "Development Plan"! Who told them to do that? They even have the gut to call that book a Five-Year Development Plan and they go and put a lot and lot of numbers in it to confuse me, as if Allah can be confused. They are confusing agents – imperialists and Zionists agents. I know what I am doing. I cannot be confused.

Mine is a Ten-Year Development Plan which I discussed and agreed with God. I can tell you this plan. Big hotels – twenty storeys – all over the country. With swimming pools, air-conditioning, large conference halls, banquet halls with my pictures all over. This will allow tourists to enjoy the hospitality of my people – that is, if I allow them to come to my land. It will allow me to enjoy myself wherever I am in my country. You see, I require good eating and good exercise, particularly in a swimming pool, in order to rest well, keep healthy and listen to God carefully every night when we communicate. These hotels must be built on high hills so that I can easily see enemies of state whenever they are approaching – and they always keep coming although they end with their heads on my lap.

My other plan is to build God's house in the capital. It just will be the tallest building so that my people can easily see and feel the presence of God. You see, I am also tall and big. Taller and bigger than all those fools put together. Yet they could not easily see and feel my presence. I also plan to build universities all over the country so that my children, whose mothers come from every part of the land, can go to universities. You see, I did not have to go to university because I am sent down on this earth by God. But my children will need to go to universities because another prophet like me will come only after another hundred years.

In my Ten-Year Plan, I am going to build airports all over the country so that I can fly from one part of the country to another in my jet and helicopters. I will build a big international airport just behind my house in my home district. It will be equipped with the most modern and sophis – sophis – ti–cate gadgets. Tourists will fly there – that is, if I allow them – to enjoy the beauty of my country. And you know what? I love driving, man, fast cars, fast driving. I need this for relaxation in-between my communication with God. So, in my plan I will build a first-class paved road to my home district to permit easy and fast cruising.

These people – my civilian Ministers – these fools – go on telling me that the country is poor, that it is underdeveloped. They are trying to confuse and deceive me by writing in long imperialist words which I cannot pronounce. They write speeches which I cannot read and which suits their interests and not mine and God's. Yet I know that the country is now rich and developed. For twelve months, when I descended on the land with full powers, I spent a great time going all over the country to open new places. I was cutting tapes weekly. That was not for nothing.

The country is developed and it is very rich. The only trouble was that all development and riches were being enjoyed by the politicians, civil servants, people of brown and white skins, all of whom are my enemies. Politicians are my enemy number one. I don't like them. I hate them. Then there are those brown people, those East Indians, who had almost all the riches of the country to themselves. They were sucking the blood of my people. My friends and I had nothing.

One of the most important thing in my Ten-Year Plan is to get rid of these people, throw them out of the country and give all their things, houses, shops, farms, factories, cars, lorries and all to my people. Then I and my people will be rich and have plenty of money. In order to make sure that my friends have plenty of money, I create my own money and put my good picture on it and produce it in any quantity. These are my Ten-Year Plan and yet these fools they tell me all sorts of non-sense – "Don't to this, don't do that otherwise the country's economy will be destroyed" – what sort of animal is this "economy"?

"The country will be poor" – as if the country has been poor. These people don't understand that I gave them the jobs to serve me and not to tell me non-sense. When they finally wake up and find that I have my plan and I am following it successfully and closely, they go out of the country and send me telegrams of resignation. Who has ever heard that Ministers resign by telegrams when out of the country! These fellows are cowards. They don't want to die for their country. I don't respect them. I respect only those people who are prepared and who die for their country. And I know a lot of them who died for their country and who are still dying. These I respect. I wish there were many thousands more of these who are prepared to die for their country.

Now because these Ministers don't understand me, I sack them and give their jobs to a new group. If these also don't understand me, I again sack them. I go on sacking them till I find the group which understand me; then we shall rule for ever and ever.

I thought it was only the Ministers who don't understand me. But alas, no! Much more than that. The Permanent Secretaries, the Under Secretaries, their Personal Secretaries, the Chairmen of State Corporations, the District Commissioners and their assistants, the Chiefs, university lecturers and students and, worse still, the masses. The masses are particularly deceptive. When I go to them they cheer up, dance, drink, sing whole night. They celebrate heavily and I like that. They give me gifts – and good gifts too – cattle, goats, sheep, shoes,

spears, bows and arrows, fresh fish from water and even their
daughters, although that takes some time. I accept these gifts
with grace and honour because I am a man of God. But the
masses are not good. As soon as I leave them they start plotting against me. They work together with my greatest enemies
– enemy number one, i.e. the politicians. They conspire with
Captain Oma and that son of a bitch, Mbuyiseni, who ran away
into hiding.

Those men! They are dirty! Not men of God. They have
managed to brainwash my people. They have no mission. I
have a mission. They are men of earth, I am a man of God. So
I must change the minds of all the people in my land. They
have been spoiled. Everywhere I go they pretend to be very
happy and give me good gifts, but deep in their hearts they see
me with bad eyes from all four directions. I know their hearts
because, as a man of God, I can read the hearts of everyone on
this earth. I know that they have been spoiled by politicians,
imperialists, Zionists and their agents. They have been brain-
washed. They can't see things my way – that is, the way of
God.

Therefore, in order to make them see things my way, I
must change them, bend those who cannot and do not want
to change. I must change these people – all of them in order to
enable me to implement my Ten-Year Plan. Actually, it is not
a Development Plan but a Plan – because we are already developed. I must change these people. That is priority number
one.

And now, how do I change the whole population to see
things my way? Simple! I have one great asset. These fools
and all the people including imperialists and Zionists and their
agents call me stupid. They call me all sorts of dirty names and
in languages which I do not understand, but my few followers
tell me all about it. I am not a fool. I am not that kind of person
whom they can call all sorts of dirty names. I know what I am
doing and I am in constant communication with Allah! How
can they beat me – a man of God! This is how I go about
changing my people.

Yes, politicians and enemies of state will be made not to see
the light of day. How is this accomplished? I will not tell the

detail because it is my secret. I do not need technical assistance for this work because I completely trained my boys in it and they are experts. In fact, I hear that leaders in other countries are seriously con – contem – thinking of asking for technical assistance from me. I will have to vet such leaders carefully before considering their requests. Anyway, I have a surplus of trained staff for this job so that there will be no problem once I approve such applications.

Those in high places who don't understand me, I shall promote them, send them on long leave and take away their jobs. Promote another group, send them on leave and take away their jobs. This procedure is repeated until those people who were put there by Captain Oma and that son of a bitch, the rogue politician, are to be removed and my people put in their place so that they may also enjoy the fruits of my reign. For those who go on leave and yet do not stay quiet and understand me and carry my orders, they also will not see the light of day. Now, some people have been trying to tell me that if I carry this out, my Government will be weak. Such people forget that for ideas, I do not need experienced and educated people. I go to God. I only need people who can understand and carry out my orders. These do not have to be highly educated and experienced. I am not educated and experienced in Government, yet I am far better than those fellows. Even God has given me a Ph.D. in Economic War. Some of the Ministers, even though they do not like me, have publicly stated that I have got natural degree in ruling.

As for the masses, three straightforward methods: (a) Pick out a few of their sons, tie them on trees and bring the rest of the people to watch my boys practise on them. Effective. They will not forget that! (b) Send out my boys for routine practice in the countryside, in the villages, in towns, etc. Effective: they will kneel before me for as long as I am around. (c) Check constantly and make sure that everyone of them get the message from the above two methods; I make my boys Provincial Governors, District Commissioners, Country Chiefs, etc. with full powers. My boys do not need to write with pens, they can write with guns. In that way, my presence will be permanently felt in the countryside where I cannot all the time be present in person.

With the above accomplished, my reorganization plan will be completed. I can then proceed to carry out my other plans. People in the foreign service, in universities, will get the message. They will begin to return to my country; otherwise they will not see the light of day. The rest of the plan will then be easy – changing names of streets, naming lakes after me, introducing official language which I can understand, putting my beautiful image on money, national flag, etc., changing the name of my country to reflect my image, changing the national anthem so that it is sung to praise me and my good work. Once these are done, I will then decree that all male children are named after me and all female children are named after my wives. At this historic moment, I will have carried out my plan. I will have achieved my objectives as ordained by God.

30 The General finished his speech to the nation, waving his forefinger in admonition. Ronald D'Mello at the back of the Conference Hall groped for his handkerchief to stuff it in his mouth and stop himself from laughing. He tripped over a television wire and fell down.

"G–bram!!" Ronald had brought a television camera down with him with a shattering roar.

"Captain Oma!" bellowed the General, diving onto the floor and pulling out his gun as he went.

"Plop – plop –plop – !"

Al Kamena dived for the floor as well. He had returned to Damibia when he realized that the press had ignored his press release and the General had not understood his public speech at the Department of Civil Bureaucracy. A bullet whistled past his ear, past where his sexual organ had been only seconds ago (he still thought of sex, even in a crisis).

There was a roar from the crowd.

"He's shot the British High Commissioner!"

"His Excellency Gould is dying!"

His Excellency, Mr. Robert Gould, popularly known as Rob, was lying in a pool of blood, his head cradled by David Michaels. Gould was moaning and Michaels was covered with blood, all the way to his forehead.

The General moved up to his knees, slowly, very slowly, as though the medals on his chest were too heavy. Captain Oma was advancing on him, growing bigger and bigger as he came closer. The bullets had missed. As the General's finger tightened on the trigger, Captain Oma reached down to the General and pulled him to his feet like a bag of empty cartridge shells. He put his hand on the General's arm and twisted the gun towards the General's head.

"No! No!" bawled the General, wrestling with the Captain to move the gun away.

"Look," gasped the crowd of dignitaries, inching backwards towards the exits. "He's crying! The General is weeping!"

Big tears were rolling down the General's cheeks. This was the first time anyone had seen him shed tears.

"I didn't mean to. Oh, Your Majesty, I didn't want..."

"He's going to shoot himself!"

As the people backed away, the gun was raised to the General's temple and the trigger was pulled. The bullet struck his head at an angle and bounced off into the photo of the Queen of England hanging on a wall. The trigger was pulled again and yet again. The General's head flew off like a missile and landed at the feet of Al Kamena. Looking like an old *mvule* tree, the headless torso of the General fell to the ground with a great thud. The floor of the great new assembly hall cracked.

EPILOGUE

Traveller

And somehow I seemed to be travelling along a long, long winding road that promised no destination; just like those red roads of my earlier years, where the dust far ahead of you told you the end was not yet.

– Ezekiel Mphahlele,
Down Second Avenue, Part Seven

I had just paid the tollgate fee and driven through the turn-pike when I saw him. Normally, I do not stop to pick up hitchhikers. You never know what crazies you may pick up in this godforsaken country of ours – some jive cat who may decide your life is worth less than the car he can take from you after stopping your breath, or maybe somebody who's decided to take out his frustrations on you. Even a micro-skirted female cannot be trusted – she may belong to some Masonic gang. So, when I see somebody walking backwards, thumb outstretched, my impulse is to tell him exactly where he can stuff that thumb.

But there was something about this cat that made me stop. He looked Puerto Rican, or Mexican, or Indian – well, he was dark. He was tall, or rather, he looked tall because he was so thin that if you pulled out a gun and shot at him he could escape the bullet by just turning aside. He had a mustache and a wispy beard – he was Mephistophelean, and he was also grinning in a Mephistophelean manner. He was dressed in a very un-American way: he was not wearing the regulation faded, dirty blue jeans, he was wearing drainpipe trousers, a white shirt, and a tie as narrow as he was. I guess that if he wore the kind of tie I was wearing, he would not have needed to wear anything else. His hand was held up in a hesitant yet confident manner. I guessed this was no cheap labourer we had imported – or who had sneaked in in accordance with the law of demand and supply – from across one of the borders.

I pulled to the side and stopped. He walked slowly up to the window, bent across the window and leaned across. I was looking into bloodshot eyes suddenly thrust close to mine. The Mephistophelean image metamorphosed into flesh and bone.

I waited for him to make a request. He said nothing. We kept looking into each other's eyes.

"Yes!" I finally said, not wanting to stay there all day, and not wanting to blow my cool at this fellow whose sole purpose in life seemed to be to lean over the window of my brand new Thunderbird.

"Can you give me a lift?" he finally said.

"A what?" I said.

"A lift," he replied. Seeing my lack of comprehension, he tried again. "A lift, a – " he made the motions of opening the door, sitting in and then said, "Zz-ooom!"

"Oh, you mean a ride! Jump right in."

"Is that what you call it in this country? I suppose you have the right to speak as you like. Since you fellows now control that little island, why should you speak the language the way those islanders say you should? So don't call it a lift, call it a ride, call it anything you like, as long as you aren't taking me for a ride."

I didn't want to puzzle that out. I opened the door. "Jump right in," I said. "The country is suffering from a fuel shortage, thanks to another round in the perpetual Middle East crisis. We have been told to conserve energy; I don't want to exhaust myself and the gas discussing semantics on the highway."

He folded his way into the auto, depositing a small bundle at his feet. He shut the door. There was a sustained high-pitched whine.

"Does your car always cry when you pick up a stranger?" he said.

"Oh," I said, "that's a new safety device. The car gives out a warning signal until you fasten the seat belt. The ends are on either side of you."

He fumbled with the belt. "Damn humanity," he said to himself as he struggled on. "So much effort to protect one life, yet so much destruction of life by making monsters leaders." I reached across to help him. Luckily the belt was not the inertia-reel type or it would have been too loose for him. I inched the auto back onto the highway.

"My name's Charlie," I said, and waited. Then I asked, "What's yours?"

"Oh," he said with a start. "Oh yes. Mine's Ronald."

"Ronald?" I said, surprised. "I thought it would be, well, anything, say Nehru, anything but Ronald!"

"Yeh," he said, and clammed up.

"Going to New York?" I finally asked.

"No," he said. "I mean, yes. Well, sort of. Actually, I'm going to Phoenix, as in the song."

"Phoenix?" I said. "Phoenix, Arizona? That's a long way off! I'm not going as far as that. When do you have to be there?"

"I'm in no hurry," he said. "I'd like to see as much of the States as I can. I don't have as much cash as I would like, so..." He raised his thumb.

"You're not from the U.S. then," I said.

"No," he said, and lapsed into a gloomy silence.

"Where are you from?" I asked. "India?"

"No," he said. Silence. Then he said, "Could I have a cigarette?"

"Sure," I said. "Help yourself. In the glove compartment."

He drew out a cigarette, inserted it between his teeth, lit it, inhaled the smoke, exhaled it through his elongated nostrils, and gave a long sigh – of relief? His hands were quivering.

"Where did you say you were from?" I asked.

"Africa," he said.

"Africa?" I turned to look at him in surprise.

"Look out!" he yelled.

I slammed the brakes. A big whump. We had smashed into it. Ah, what the heck! It was not my fault that the dog had decided to run across the highway at that point. I changed into second and started accelerating.

"Stop!" he barked. "We must go back and see." Rather than argue, I stopped, moved to the side, and parked. We got out and walked all the way back. The thing was lying on the ground. It had been a beautiful black Alsatian. Its skull was open and the brains had spilled out. There was blood and stuff all over the place. I could not bear to walk up to it and dragged my feet.

"Poor dog," I heard him say. "Just your luck you happened to be at the wrong place at the wrong time. What made you cross the road when you should have been running away from it as fast as you could, far from the murderous machines of people!"

After all my caution, I had picked up a weirdo! I considered leaving him there to deliver his philosophical eulogy on the dog and sneaking away, but he got up just at that moment and started walking back. As he walked past me, I heard him say to himself, "No life, however insignificant, should pass away without at least being noticed."

The next few miles were covered in silence while I thought of those African novels of Graham Greene in which cars were always killing dogs. If that was so common in Africa, why was he so upset?

"Yes," he said, startling me. I began to suspect he could read my mind. "I come from Africa. Why does everybody assume I come from India?" He gave a dry laugh. "To be precise, I have been thrown out of Africa." He threw back his head and laughed again, if that scraping of two pieces of sandpaper could be called a laugh. I was regretting having given him a ride. I had forgotten that other countries had their share of crazies as well. Living in this vast, troubled, chauvinistic country, one often has no idea what is really going on elsewhere.

Hesitantly, I said, "Thrown out? Why?"

"God knows," he said, laughing again. "I mean that literally. The army officer running Damibia – the country I was thrown out of – woke up one day and said that God had spoken to him. God must be fed up of all the good people He has in heaven with Him because He seems these days to speak only to the brutes. Anyway, God told him to throw out all the brown people – Indians – from Damibia. Being God-fearing, he threw us out, of course."

I didn't know what to say. This country would never throw people out *en masse* because all of us were foreigners here, so to speak. Except the Indians. I mean the Amerindians.

"But dammit, why did he have to kill so many people!"

I saw his bony knuckles squashing the second cigarette he had lit. "You mean, he killed brown people, Indians, East Indians, after telling them to go?"

"No! I mean, yes! Oh hell – I don't know what I'm saying. Look, there were about 120,000 brown people in a country of 13 million. He killed, I don't know, about 500 Indians. He has killed – he and his thugs – about 150,000 Africans, black people. Well, you work out the statistics. But in absolute terms... "

"Look," I said, "we're coming into New York City. Have you been here before?"

"Well, in a way. I arrived at Kennedy Airport at night and drove that very night to New Haven in blinding rain."

"By bus?"

"No, by limousine."

I smiled.

"What's so funny?" he asked.

"Well," I said, "in this country, only V.I.P.s travel by limousine. It's funny to think of a refugee from one country being a V.I.P. in another! Of course, I had forgotten that the airport had a limousine service."

We were approaching New York City. The skyscrapers could be seen.

"God, look at those monsters!" he said.

"What monsters?"

"Those high-rise buildings. I first saw them in Canada, in Toronto."

"Don't you have any buildings where you come from? Oh, I forgot, it was Africa."

"Blast it, do you think that people in Africa live in a jungle?"

"Sorry!" I said. "I only know what I've seen in films."

Silence.

"You said you were in Canada," I said. "What were you doing there?"

"Looking up some of my people," he said, meditatively. "Canada accepted most of them."

"How are they?"

"Same as before. But worse than before. Some feel regret, pain at having left. All are consumed by the consumer jungle. And even more divided, resentful of those who own bigger cars, bigger houses ... junk, that's what they live for! I should have joined the guerillas ..." He tapered off.

"What guerillas?"

"Oh well, guerillas. They are the same all over. Is that the Empire State Building, the tallest one in the world?"

"No more," I said. "About the tallest are those gray twin towers, the World Trade Center."

"Wow!" he said. "This country must have the greatest money can buy. Looks like the Tower of Babel, reaching up into the heavens."

"Where are you going?" I asked.

"Nowhere in particular," he said.

"Would you like a drink?" I said.

"Great," he said. "But I warn you – I don't have any *pesa*."

"What's that?"

"The thing that makes this country go round. Moola, bread, dough, cash. Money, my friend. What you use to find friends in Latin America, Africa and other countries. Never showing that I could be such a friend, I have never had much of the stuff, but leaving Africa like I did, I have even less."

"Oh, that's all right!" I said. "I know a small restaurant and bar. There are some small restaurants in this huge city."

"Of course," he said. "The small people must survive in the kinks of the walls of the rich and the powerful."

This was a strange fellow. Was he a leftist or Communist? The country was full of them. But they were the most unlikable, stupid, lazy bums one could ever meet. At least, that's what was said. I had never actually met one. Maybe this was my chance. He may have been thrown out of his country for being just that.

We were driving along 42nd Street. We had stopped at the lights for the dozenth time when he said, "Hey, what's with this road? Why can't we just drive straight? Why so many lights? Why is the road so full of ups and downs?"

Those were damed foolish questions so I didn't answer them.

"Hey, look at all those overgrown crabs! Look at those Colossi, out to grab us! No wonder so many Americans develop paranoia and go completely berserk, climbing some tower or other to shoot at everybody!"

"Wait a minute!" I said, my patriotism rising. It was usually quiescent. There was little enough to praise this country for, what with its violence, garbage, pollution and corruption. But when a refugee – mind you, a refugee who had been thrown out of his own country and had been generously accepted by this country – when this country was good enough to accept him, how dare he criticize it?

I was about to say something shattering when he said, "These buildings remind me of the Colossi of Memnon, which

I saw near Luxor in Egypt about a year ago. They are equally tall and brooding. But the Colossi, built thousands of years ago by a civilized Non-White race, though ruthlessly feudal, look human. Well, they are like gigantic sculptures of human beings so they must look human. What I mean is that these buildings are impersonal, monstrous, blank. Wonder what people five thousand years from now will think about them? What if we are all wiped out, if one of the H-Bomb planes goes out of control, as in *Dr. Strangelove*; what will our mutant descendants make of the Empire State Building?"

We had turned up 51st Street, and now we would face the problem of parking. God knows what madman thought of building these monstrous autos without making sure that we could find a place to park them in New York. But I was lucky – somebody ahead was just pulling out so I stopped behind him.

"You're lucky this isn't Cairo!" he said. "By now, a million horns would be sounding behind you. At least in this respect, New York is civilized. Though I suppose it is better to take out your frustrations by hooting your horn than by killing – what is the New York rate? – three people a day?"

I was now preoccupied with squeezing the Thunderbird into a small space and only hissed. Besides, that was probably the correct figure.

"C'mon," I said. We got out and walked up the street.

"Man, look at the way the people dress!" he said. "No wonder so many women are raped in this country every day!"

Hold on now! This was beginning to get to me! But before I could speak, he continued, "Still, I suppose it's better to let people dress as they wish. In my country – ex-country – the Leader, the Great One ordained by God, the General who grabbed power with a gun in order to Restore Democracy to the country, decided in his great wisdom to ban the wearing of miniskirts. And so a law was promulgated, making it illegal to wear clothes with hemlines three inches above the kneeline. And then all hell broke loose. What was the kneeline? The top of the kneecap? The bottom? The middle? Did you discover the kneecap by letting women stand up, sit down, or kneel?"

I laughed. Those dictators of the banana republics were all the same, whether they were Latin American or African.

"I was fined one day for wearing a mini," he said.

"What?" I said. "Do you have Scots ancestors?"

"No," he said, smiling fiendishly. "I discovered that the law did not specify that miniskirts were dresses worn by women so I wore the shortest shorts I could find, just to find out what would happen. I was arrested, of course. I thought that I could use my training in law in India to fight my case out and show how absurd the whole law was."

"What happened?"

"The day before my case came up, the army thugs grabbed the Chief Justice from his office in broad daylight and allegedly chopped his head off. I decided it was better to plead guilty than to challenge the law, such as it was. I only qualified my plea by saying that I was going out to do some jogging, so I was let off with just a warning and a fine."

By now, we had reached Hungry Pete's. We went in and sat at the counter. "Hey, Pete," I called out to the barman.

"Charlie!" he said. "Charlie Cash himself!" He came over to give me a bone-crunching handshake.

"Pete, let me introduce my friend Ronald."

"Hi, Ron," said Pete.

"Where are you from, India?"

The smile from Ronald's face dimmed as he said, "Africa."

"No kidding!" said Pete.

"Yes!" said Ronald. "I'm from Africa. But I'm not African. Or am I? God knows what I am! But what I am right now is thirsty."

"Oh wow! I'm forgetting my Brooklyn hospitality!" said Pete. "What will you have?"

"Michelob, since you are offering it," I said.

"Any draft beer for me," said Ronald.

"Coming up!" said Pete, passing two beer mugs on to us. I was reaching for my billfold but Pete said, "No, Charlie boy, this one is on the house to make Ron feel at home. If he doesn't know what he is, why, let him learn that he has a home in America. Like me, like you, Charlie boy."

"Cheers!" said Ronald, taking a swig.

"Where did you say you came from – Brooklyn?" Ronald was asking Pete.

"Yeah, that's where I live. Do you know it?"

"I've not been there, but who doesn't know Brooklyn? That's where all your famous writers come from – Norman Mailer, Paule Marshall, Arthur Miller, and others."

"I've heard of Mailer," said Pete. "He's the boozy guy who tried to run for mayor a few years back. Pity he lost. He would have been good for business."

"How come you know our writers?" I asked.

"Because I make it my business to learn the tricks of the trade."

"You mean you're a writer?"

"Yes, I mean no. I mean in a way. What I mean is that I worked in the Damibian Ministry of Public Information, Radio Division, so, like a good information man, I keep in touch. I also write various things to inform people about what is happening."

"Have you written anything since coming here?" I asked.

"Well – I don't feel at ease in this violent country, and you need to feel relaxed to write."

"If so, why are you travelling around so trustingly accepting rides from strangers? Why, maybe I would cut your throat and throw you off onto the highway!"

Ronald scowled, then laughed. "There is also a generous streak in the American people, a survival of the pioneer spirit. It accepted me! The other day, an old lady in New Haven heard that I was a refugee. She immediately sent me sixteen new shirts! They were too loose, of course."

"All this time, you only made offensive remarks about this country," I said.

"I don't know this country well enough yet," he said. "It was built on violence, something I have had to live with. Immigrants, fleeing from inhospitable Europe, stole the land from the Indians and Mexicans, stole labour from Africans and Chinese. That is violence enough. It is suppressed, hidden, not out in the open. Until it erupts."

I began to get angry again. This refugee had a nerve being so critical when he had been thrown out of an incomparably more violent country, from what he said.

Maybe to appease me, he smiled and said, "Anyway, I'll show you what I have written since I arrived." He took out a grubby pile of handwritten pages. "This is an attempt by a non-violent man to deal with a violent world."

"I can't read in this light," I said, straining my eyes. "Can I read it at our hotel?" I had decided to be generous and pay the motel accommodation for Ronald for the night.

"We-e-e-ll ..." he said, doubtfully.

"Look," I said, "I have connections with the literary business, with agents and magazines. I will see if the material is promising, if it is publishable."

"Well, why not?" he said. "The story must be told some day."

That night, I read *Spiralling, The General Is Up*, a novel by Ronald D'Cruz. It was a most incredible story, what I could read of it. There were several paragraphs of gory descriptions of murders which had been deleted, along with the deletion of some names. It seemed like a work of fantasy or a draft horror film-script. But it was promising, I thought. I couldn't put it down until I had finished. But it would need work and some editing.

In the morning, I looked for Ronald. He wasn't there. I checked with the receptionist. Ronald had checked out.

"Didn't he say anything?"

"Mumbled something about joining gorillas or something."

So he was gone, leaving me, the son of a Lebanese immigrant, with the handwritten pages of an exotic novel about Africa.

History is sometimes changed by idiots. -Ali Shalash

Glossary

NOTE: Swahili and Luganda vowels are pronounced as follows:
a – like "a" in "father"
e – like "a" - in say, but flat and without a "diphthong" at the end
i – like - "e" in "be"
o – like - "o" in "ho! ho!"
u – like - "oo" in "too"
Generally, the sound of the vowel in a stressed syllable is the same as that in an unstressed tone.
The sound of "n" is like the first "n" in "condone".
(Strictly speaking, "Swahili" should be "Kishwahili".)

Apartheid *(Afrikaans)* – South African policy of separate development of the races. In practice, and with the aid of a legal machine, the Non-White people are to be hewers of wood and the drawers of water for all time while the White people are to be privileged.

Arusi (Swahili) – wedding, marriage.

Ayah (Swahili) – maidservant, governess.

Baksisi ("Pidgin" Swahili, from Arabic) – monetary gift in appreciation of services rendered.

Busuti (Luganda) – African woman's dress, said to have been designed by a Goan tailor named Gomes (and so an alternate name for the dress is *Gomisi*) on the instructions of a Victorian lady missionary teacher, who was shocked at the flimsy clothing of a pupil. It has high sleeves and a bustle.

Boot (British English) – trunk of car.

Bwana (Swahili) – bossman.

Duka (Swahili, originally from an Indian language) – small, all-purpose shop.

Dukawalla – shopkeeper.

Fagia jumbani ("Ki-settla", i.e., Settler or "Pidgin" Swahili) – sweep the house.

Feinim or *feni* (Konkani) – potent Goan alcoholic drink made from cashew fruit.

Cheque (British English); check (American). Under the British banking system in Africa, cancelled cheques (i.e., after the bank has cleared them) are not returned to the customer.

Goa – a state on the western seaboard of India, covering an area of about 3,700 square kilometres, including ten rivers and fifteen islands. At the time the book was written, the population of Goa was about 900,000, of which 59 percent were Hindus, 38 percent Roman Catholics and 2 percent Muslims. Now, approximately 1.6 million. Goa was ruled by the Portuguese from 1510 to 1961. The indigenous language of the Goans is Konkani, derived from a Prakritic form of Sanskrit. It had, and continues to have, a large diasporic population. In the ex-British colonies of East and Central Africa, almost all Goans were Roman Catholics who spoke English as a first language, though some of them freely throw in Konkani and Swahili words or expressions.

Hospitali ("Pidgin" Swahili) – hospital.

Jambo (Swahili) – hello.

Kali (Swahili) – hot, pungent, sharp.

Kilabu ("Pidgin" Swahili) – club, institute.

Kitenge (Swahili) – colourful material of cotton, used to make shirts like *dashikis* or dresses or skirts. It has special designs on each piece.

Kondo (Luganda) – violent robber or thug.

Ko ona rafiki ("Pidgin" Swahili) – to see a friend.

Kuja ("Pidgin" Swahili) – come.

Kwaheri (Swahili) – goodbye.

Laeta chai ("Ki-settla" Swahili) – bring tea.

Lorry (British English) – truck.

Masala (Konkani) – mixture of spices, prepared by grinding on a black grinding stone with a black roller and used for making Goan curry.

Matoke (Luganda) – fruit like plantain or banana, which is cooked.

Memsahib (Swahili) – madam.

Mingi (Swahili) – many.

Mugoa (Swahili) – Goan/s.

Muindi (strictly "Muhindi") (Swahili) – Indian/s.

Mungu (Swahili) – God.

Muzungu (strictly "Mzungu") (Swahili) White man.

Mvule (Swahili) – a strong tree, in size and strength comparable to the oak.

Mwenge (Luganda) – potent alcoholic drink.

Nosib (Konkani) – fate.

Ndege (Swahili) – bird, plane.

Pesa (Swahili, from an Indian language) – money.

Petrol (British English) – gas.

Pisi ("Ki-settla" or "Pidgin" Swahili) – cook.

Potato crisps (British English) – potato chips.

Queue (British English) – line of people.

Rafiki (Swahili) – friend.

Sababu apana fagia jumbani ("Ki-settla" Swahili) — Why haven't you swept the house?

Samaki (Swahili) – fish.

Shamba (Swahili) – garden.

Simama (Swahili) – stand, stop.

Ugali (Swahili) - a kind of porridge, something like grits.

Wacha (Swahili) – leave it.

Wapi (Swahili) – where.

Watu (Luganda) – people.

PETER NAZARETH is Professor of English and Advisor to the International Writing Program at the University of Iowa. Born in Uganda of Goan parentage, he obtained his honours degree in English from Makerere University College.

He worked in the Ministry of Finance, where he was Senior Finance Officer when he left in 1973 to accept the Seymour Lustman Fellowship at Yale University, granted because of his first novel, *In a Brown Mantle*, which was prophetic of the Asian Expulsion from Uganda by Idi Amin. From Yale, he was invited to be an Honorary Fellow in the International Writing Program and to teach African Literature in the African American Studies Program at the University of Iowa.

His publications include *Literature and Society in Modern Africa* (published by Northwestern University Press as *An African View of Literature*), *Two Radio Plays, The Third World Writer: His Social Responsibility, In the Trickster Tradition: The Novels of Andrew Salkey, Francis Ebejer and Ishmael Reed, A fény felé* (Budapest: Europa, 1984) and *Edwin Thumboo: Creating a Nation Through Poetry*.

His criticism and fiction have appeared in several anthologies and journals. He has edited *African Writing Today*, an issue of *Pacific Quarterly Moana*, and *Goan Literature: A Modern Reader*, an issue of the *Journal of South Asian Literature*, and *Critical Essays on Ngugi wa Thiong'o*. Three of his plays were broadcast by the British Broadcasting Corporation. He was President of the African Literature Association and also Chair of the African-American World Studies Program.

Goa 1556

Catalogue 2013

GOANA / LOCAL STUDIES

■ *As Dear As Salt* (Reyna Sequeira). Goa was once famous for its salt. This book is authored by a researcher who has focussed on this topic since 1992 and did her Ph.D on salt-farming communities in three villages (Agarvaddo in Pernem, Batim in Tiswadi and Arpora in Bardez). ISBN 978-93-80739-61-8 Rs 400

■ *Goa – Found and Imagined: Possibilities, potentials, tips and tools.* Students of a post-master's inter-disciplinary course in urbanism from Sweden encounter Goa. They ask the question: "Could urbanisation propose other ways of interpreting the prevailing spirit between nature and culture?" They come up with an insightful take on contemporary Goan society. With the Royal Institute of Art, Sweden. ISBN 978-93-80739-63-2 Rs 200

■ *Goa: Folklore Studies* (P. Phaldesai ISBN 978-93-80739-22-9 Rs. 295. Pp 280)

■ *Mapusa: Yesterday and Today – A Reminiscent Tour* (Domnic P.F. Fernandes. ISBN 978-93-80739-43-4 Rs 350. 2012.)

■ *Land of the Sal Tree: Stories of the history, legends and traditions of Saligao, a typical Goan village.* (Fr Nascimento J. Mascarenhas Illus: Mel D'Souza ISBN 978-93-80739-35-9 312 pp. Rs 350) A book on Saligao village.

■ *Beyond the Beach: The Village of Arossim, Goa, in Historical Perspective* (T D'Silva ISBN 978-93-80739-10-6 Rs. 195 Pp 176.)

■ *Picture-Postcard Poverty: Unheard voices, forgotten issues from rural Goa* (Mani/Noronha ISBN 978-81-905682-8-9 Rs. 150. Pp 130. Pb.)

■ *Another Goa* (Frederick Noronha ISBN 978-81-90568-27-2 Rs. 245. Pp 192. Pb.)

■ *Domnic's Goa* (Domnic Fernandes ISBN 978-81-904640-0-0 Rs. 350. Pp 264.)

MIGRATION

■ *Colonialism, Migration and the International Catholic Goan Community* (S. Mascarenhas-Keyes ISBN 978-93-80739-31-1 Rs. 395.)

■ *Goan Pioneers in Bombay* (Teresa Albuquerque ISBN 978-93-80739-23-6 Rs 295)

■ *Into the Diaspora Wilderness* (Selma Carvalho ISBN 978-93-80739-02-1 282 pp. Rs. 345.) Looks at Goan migration in the English speaking world. 2e.

■ *Songs of the Surviors* (Yvonne Vaz-Ezdani ISBN 978-81-905682-4-1 Rs. 295. Pp 290. Pb.) The story of Goans in Burma in 1942.

■ *The Last Prabhu: A hunt for roots -- DNA, ancient documents and migration in Goa* (Bernardo Elvino de Sousa ISBN 978-93-80739-15-1 Rs. 195. Pp 172. Pb.)

BIOGRAPHY

■ *It's Been A Long Day: A Nonagenarian Remembers* (Irene Heredia, ISBN 978-93-80739-44-1, Pp 144. Rs 195, 2012.)

■ *Goa's Liberation and Thereafter: Chronicles of a Fragmented Life* (Suresh Kanekar 978-93-80739-30-4 Rs. 295. Pp 276. Pb.)

■ *Everything is Grace. The Diary of an International Immigrant Priest.* George Aranha. ISBN 978-93-80739-54-0. Rs 400.

■ *Battles Waged, Lasting Dreams* (Silvia Braganca ISBN 978-93-80739-19-9 Rs. 350. Pp 560 Pb.) On Aquino Braganza, who fought for the cause of Black Africa.

■ *Patriotism in Action: Goans In India's Defence Services* (Valmiki Faleiro ISBN 978-93-80739-06-9 Rs. 600. Pp 344. Pb.)

■ *Mansion of Glass: The GKB Story* (K.G. Gupta ISBN 978-93-80739-08-3 Rs. 400)

■ *Girls in Green: Memories from St Mary's* (ISBN 978-81-90568-22-7 Rs. 120. Pp 116.)

MUSIC/THEATRE

■ *Undra Muja Mama Folk Songs of Goa: An Anthology of Dulpods* (Dr Jose Pereira, Micael Martins, Antonio Costa ISBN 978-93-80739-26-7 Pp 220. Pb. Rs. 295.)

■ *Song of Goa Crown of Mandos* (same authors as above, Pp 496. Hb. ISBN 978-93-80739-03-8 Rs. 550.)

■ *When the Curtains Rise* (Andre Rafael Fernandes ISBN 978-93-80739-01-4 Rs. 195. Pp 216. Pb.) On the *tiatr*, a vibrant form of modern Indian theatre from Goa.

HISTORY

■ *Medieval Goa: A Socio-Economic History* (Teotonio R de Souza Rs. 395 pb. Rs 495 hb.)

LITERATURE / GOAN WRITING

■ *Oriente e Ocidente na Literatura Goesa* (Dr Eufemiano de Jesus Miranda ISBN 978-93-80739-24-3 328 pp. Rs 395) A detailed study of Goan writing in Portuguese.

■ *Modern Goan Literature Pivoting On the Point of Return: An Anthology* (Peter Nazareth (ed.) ISBN 978-81-90568-25-8 Rs. 395. Pp 478. Pb.) Fascinating early anthology.

■ *Mirror to Goa* (Donna J Young ISBN 978-81-90568-21-0 Rs. 195. Pp 178. Pb.) An American look at the work of Goan fiction.

■ *Francisco Luis Gomes 1829-1869 A Select Reader* (Luis Assis Correia, ed. ISBN 978-93-80739-28-1 Rs. 350 pb Rs 500 hb. Pp 456.)

Includes full-text translation of the novel *Os Brahamanes*.

RELIGION / ART / CHRISTIANITY

■ *Written in Stone: Jesuit buildings in Goa and their artistic and architectural features.* (Cristina Osswald. ISBN 978-93-80739-16-8 Pp 400 Rs 400)

■ *Passion in Paradise: Modern Day Catholicism in Goa* (Christina Fernandes. ISBN 978-93-80739-46-5 Pp 80. Hb. Colour. Rich in photographs. Rs 250)

TRAVELOGUE

■ *My Journeys Through Wonderland* (Brenda Rodrigues ISBN 978-93-80739-37-3 436 pp. Rs 450.) Accounts of an avid globetrotter.

MEDIA

■ *In Black and White: Insiders' Stories about the press in Goa* (ISBN 978-81-905682-0-3 Rs. 195.) Looks at the media over four decades.

LAW

■ *Right to Information: A Step-by-Step Guidebook* (N Sahai & V Rajgadia ISBN 978-93-80739-39-7 200 pp. Rs 295) 2e.

CRAFT

■ *The Art of Coconut Craft* (Vijaydatta Lotlikar ISBN 978-81-90568-23-4 Rs. 195.)

MISCELLANEOUS

■ *The Rise of India* (Eugenio Monteiro ISBN 978-93-80739-20-5 Rs. 295. Pp 352. Pb.)

■ *Stay Safe, Cybercitizen!* (Lucius Lobo, Illustrated by Vijay Kumar Kakade. ISBN 978-93-80739-29-8 Rs 200)

■ *Follow Me: Volume III* (Fr Nascimento J. Mascarenhas ISBN 978-93-80739-00-7 Rs. 345 hb. Pp xx + 428.) Details on the churches of Salcete and Mormugao.

FICTION

■ *Stray Mango Branches.... (short stories).* Fatima Noronha. ISBN 978-93-80739-59-5. Rs 200. Charming short stories and reminiscences "with Goan sap". Rs 200

■ *The General Is Up.* Peter Nazareth's powerful novel set in Africa. (ISBN 978-93-80739-65-6 176pp. Rs 200)

■ *Just Matata: A Novel Set in Kenya and Goa* (Braz Menezes ISBN 978-93-80739-36-6 304 pp. Rs 295)

■ *A Matter of Time.* Brenda Coutinho ISBN 978-93-80739-58-8. Going down memory lane and reminding us what it was like growing up in a village in the Goa of the 1980s. Rs 200.

■ *Consequences.* By Nigel Fernandes. A suspense-thriller. ISBN 978-93-80739-62-5 Rs 200

■ *Puck y los Mil y Un Sueños de un Solstico de Verano: Una Historia Magica de Goa* (In Spanish. Ana Machado de Dios. ISBN 978-93-80739-53-3) Also as *Puck and the Thousand and One Midsummer Dreams: A Magical History of Goa* (Ana Machado de Dios ISBN 978-93-80739-52-6 Rs 495. Hb. Pp 220) Ebook versions.

■ *Pirates! Beware!* (Capt. Norbert Rebello ISBN 978-93-80739-34-2 342 pp. Rs 395)

■ *The Cry of the Kingfisher* (Belinda Viegas ISBN 978-93-80739-13-7 Rs. 195. Pb.)

■ *Shades Within Shadows:* (Alan Machado ISBN 978-93-80739-32-8 Rs. 350. Pp 276.)

■ *The Tulsi... and other Short Stories from Goa* (Edila Gaitonde ISBN 978-93-80739-25-0 Rs. 195) Stories of Goa.

■ *Inside/Out: New Writing from Goa.* (J. Lourenco/H. Dirkin, eds. Rs. 195. ISBN 978-93-80739-11-3)

■ *Goa Masala An Anthology of Stories by Canadian Goans* (Ben Antao, ed. ISBN 978-93-80739-04-5 Rs. 195. Pp 272. Pb.)

■ *Skin. A Novel.* (Margaret Mascarenhas ISBN 978-93-80739-05-2 Rs. 295.)

■ *The Sting of Peppercorns: A novel* (Antonio Gomes ISBN 978-81-90568-29-6 Rs. 295. Pp 296.)

■ *Off-side* (John Aguiar ISBN 978-93-80739-09-0) *The Perfect Match* (Maria de Lima Pereira ISBN 978-93-80739-09-0 Rs. 99 Pb.)

CHILDREN'S

■ *Fuloos Plays with the Sun* (Angela Ferrao, 12 pp, colour, Rs 50). A colourful story about a baby camel. Ideal for 6 years and below.

■ *Espi Mai Is Stuck Again and Other Goan Tales* (Anita Pinto ISBN 978-93-80739-56-4. Rs. 195. Pp 148. Pb.) Charming short stories, for 5 to 11 year olds, all set in Goa.

■ Also in Konkani as *Espi May Porot Xirkoli ani Goycheo her kannio* (ISBN 978-93-80739-55-7 Rs. 195. Pp 144.

■ *The Golden Gate and other stories* is a set of delightful tales for everyone. Rs 195.

CUISINE

■ *Cozinha de Goa: history and tradition of Goan food* (Fátima da Silva Gracias ISBN 978-93-80739-40-3 Rs. 295.) The definitive work on the history of Goan food. 2e

■ *Goan Recipes and More* (Odette Mascarenhas ISBN 978-93-908116-5-9 Rs. 399. Pp 238. Pb.) Printed fully in colour.

■ *Delights of Goa* (Alda Figueiredo ISBN 978-93-80739-21-2. Rs. 195. Pp 162. Pb. Large size.) Lovely book of Goan recipies.

■ *Kornelia's Kitchen: Mediterranean Cooking for India* (Kornelia Santoro ISBN 978-93-80739-07-6 Rs. 295)

POETRY

■ *Mirrorred Reflections* by Antonio Gomes (forthcoming). ISBN 978-93-80739-64-9 Poetry. Rs 200.

■ *Whispers of the Heart* (Capt N. Rebello, ISBN 978-93-80739-38-9 64pp hb. Rs 195)

FORTHCOMING

■ *Globalising Goa* (1660-1820) (Ernestine Carreira) A rich account by a scholar in Paris of the place Goa occupied in India and the world beyond, before the advent of the British Raj. It was the capital of an European maritime empire that teetered on the brink of collapse in the tumultuous 17th century, only to become a thriving cultural, religious and diplomatic hub in the 18th century, building close relations with the foremost continental empires of the day -- Mogul, Maratha and Mysore. ISBN 978-93-80739-60-1. Pp 650.

■ *Bomoicar.* Journalist Reena Martins talks to people across the generations to piece together a story of the Goa that lived in, and encountered, Bombay.

■ *Re-Figuring Goa: From Trading Post to Tourism Destination.* Challenging our current understanding of Goan society and history. Raghu Trichur.

We do mail-order to any part of the globe, and can send you an estimate of the costs for despatching books, single titles or in bulk, to anywhere. Registered airmail from India works out reasonable, effective and safe and can reach in 14-20 days of ordering. Speedy delivery via courier available at extra costs.

Our books are stocked at the main bookshops of Goa and in libraries across the State.
Visit us to buy direct or mail order from Goa,1556 at Saligão 403511 Bardez Goa. (Nearest landmark: Lourdes Convent, Sonarbhat, Saligao). Contacts goa1556@gmail.com +91-9822122436 or +91-832-2409490. Online, check Amazon.com or itsallhere.in Contact us if you would like to stock our titles.

Our latest catalogue is at http://www.scribd.com/doc/76671049/Goa1556-Catalogue-Books-from-Goa

Join the Goa,1556 Book Club and get a 30% discount on our prices within Goa or special discounts on purchase of three or more books when ordered from overseas, besides detailed information about our latest and forthcoming publications via email. Membership on payment of a one-time fee of Rs 500 (US$15) by crossed-cheque favouring Goa,1556.

Interested in keeping in touch with the informative world of Goa-related books? Sign up at this Goa,1556-initiated active e-mailing list:
http://groups.google.com/group/ goa-book-club